DASTARDLY DEEDS AT ST BRIDE'S

A GEMMA LAMB COSY MYSTERY

DEBBIE YOUNG

Boldwood

First published in Great Britain in 2019. This edition first published by Boldwood Books Ltd in 2022.

Copyright © Debbie Young, 2019

Cover Design by Lawston Design

Cover Photography: Shutterstock

The moral right of Debbie Young to be identified as the author of this work has been asserted in accordance with the Copyright, Designs and Patents Act 1988.

Every effort has been made to obtain the necessary permissions with reference to copyright material, both illustrative and quoted. We apologise for any omissions in this respect and will be pleased to make the appropriate acknowledgements in any future edition.

A CIP catalogue record for this book is available from the British Library.

Paperback ISBN 978-1-80483-032-1

Large Print ISBN 978-1-80483-028-4

Hardback ISBN 978-1-80483-027-7
Ebook ISBN 978-1-80483-025-3

Kindle ISBN 978-1-80483-026-0

Audio CD ISBN 978-1-80483-033-8

MP3 CD ISBN 978-1-80483-030-7

Digital audio download ISBN 978-1-80483-024-6

Boldwood Books Ltd
23 Bowerdean Street
London SW6 3TN
www.boldwoodbooks.com

To my past partners in staffroom crime

It's not academic qualifications
	that make the world worth living in.
	It's human kindness.

— MISS HARNETT,

— HEADMISTRESS OF ST BRIDE'S SCHOOL
FOR GIRLS

PROLOGUE
OCTOBER

What on earth was that circling her neck? And how could something so long have fitted in a trouser pocket?

The distinctive smell provided a clue – the thick, sickly scent of rubber, like car tyres. Her mother had always liked the smell of rubber, associating it with hospitals. Life-saving in that setting, but intended to be life-taking now.

Or was it only meant to give her a fright? Was it some kind of game? Well, she could play games too. If she played dead, her attacker might back off, loosen the tube restricting her air. In any case, she was too tired to put up a fight.

She let her hands fall limp at her sides. If only she had a little more air, she'd be fighting fit. Like the clear, pure air of a stroll through the school gardens perhaps; with more than an acre of garden per girl, St Bride's never had any shortage of fresh air.

Never mind a stroll; right now she felt she might just float away. What a lightweight she was! Or did she mean low mass?

What was the difference between weight and mass again? The head of science would know. She ought to ask.

That's where she'd last smelt rubber: in the science lab. Bunsen burner tubes were made of rubber. Detach one of those from its burner and gas tap, and it would easily fit in a trouser pocket. You could coil it up like a pet snake. A trouser snake. But was this one a harmless grass snake or a lethal boa constrictor?

Was that her pulse she could feel, or the snake's? Snakes might be cold-blooded, but they'd still have a pulse.

Her eyes were hurting now. Of course they were; she still had her contact lenses in. She must take them out before she fell asleep, or she'd look like she'd been drinking all night. What a bad example that would set for the girls!

Perhaps it was time to stop playing games and yell for help. But if she did, would anyone hear her through these thick old walls of Cotswold stone?

As the pressure at her throat eased for a moment, she took her chance, sucking in enough oxygen, in a vast, noisy gasp, to fuel at least one scream. Yes, and a well-aimed kick. She'd show them just who was boss.

The second scream was not her own but she didn't care. Mission accomplished, she passed out cold, contact lenses and all.

1

FLAT CHANCE

September

Perching on the vast sofa in the school's great entrance hall at the appointed time of midday, I realised the room was bigger than our entire flat.

I say our flat. Steven's flat, actually, since I'd just moved out. Technically it had been his all along, but after the first few months, he'd allowed me to call it ours.

Moving in with Steven had been a mistake. But now at last I had made my bid for freedom, and I was about to move into a place of my own. Well, sort of my own. My teaching post at St Bride's School for Girls came with accommodation, which would be mine for as long as I could hold down the job. I confess the staff flat had been the main reason I'd applied.

But I wasn't about to get tied down long-term again. This time I was committed for only a year, and an academic one at that – September till July. There was also a faster escape route if I needed one: until my probationary term was over, my contract might be curtailed at a month's notice on either side.

Perhaps all live-in relationships should start out on those terms.

Nervous as I was of taking up my new job, it seemed a better option than my only alternative: returning to live with my parents. It wasn't so much that at the age of thirty I felt too old to go back home. The trouble was we'd fallen out over Steven. Everyone but my parents found him charming. 'Ooh, he's a keeper,' my friends told me, and I was foolish enough to believe them.

I was therefore determined to make this new job work. Admittedly there were complications, such as my never having worked as a teacher before. But I had a degree in English and a post-graduate teaching qualification, and fond memories of my own schooldays that might make returning to the class-room feel like a homecoming.

And St Bride's School for Girls was stunning – not a bit like the state secondary school that I'd attended. The former stately home of one of the richest gentlemen in Victorian England, it was nationally recognised for its historical and architectural significance. Wrapped around the mansion was an immense private estate of beautiful gardens and parkland, isolating it from the real world. It felt like an upmarket nunnery.

And like a nunnery, my new home would keep me safe from any more unsuitable romances, for the simple reason that there were no men on site. As the staff list in the prospectus made clear, St Bride's only employed women.

To be honest, a nunnery was about the only escape route from my dependence on Steven that I hadn't considered. I'd bluffed my way through various interviews for everything from live-in carer to chambermaid. I'd even thought of applying to be a lighthouse keeper, fancying the idea of living in my own little fortress with its cosy curved rooms, safe from all intruders, and only the sea for company. I'd been disappointed to discover the role was now entirely automated. On balance, a residential teaching post was much more appropriate. At least it was something I might actively enjoy, once I'd conquered my nerves...

Now, gazing up at the marble columns to the ornately-painted, domed ceiling, where chubby cherubs circuited the heavens above me, I felt the size of an ant – and about as likely to be crushed underfoot by the next passer-by. After living with Steven, my confidence was not at its peak. Yet for the first time in seven years, I was calling the shots in my personal life. The responsibility was intoxicating – and not a little terrifying as my contract clearly stated that I was on a term's probation. I was glad to be in a safe, secluded place at last, and desperate that it should not be snatched away from me if I put a foot wrong.

A tapping noise interrupted my thoughts. Just starting to descend the sweeping staircase at the far end of the hall was an elegant young woman of about my age with eyes like polished jet. She flashed a taut smile as she stepped lightly and rhythmically down the broad marble stairs, perfectly equidistant from the swirling, wrought iron bannisters on either side. For a moment, I thought she was going to break into a Busby Berkeley routine, with men in top hats and tails springing out from the shadows to tap-dance down in her wake. If it had been me walking down that gleaming staircase, I'd have been clinging on for dear life to the handrail, even in my habitual flat shoes. How she managed to stay upright in a pencil skirt and black stilettos as shiny as her glossy black bob was beyond me.

Having reached the foot of the stairs, she marched purposefully towards me across the antique Persian rug that gave the only touch of warmth to the hall. Even on this sunny early-September day, the chill air nipped at my flesh. Now I understood why the school uniform list in the prospectus included thermal underwear.

When she held out a perfectly manicured hand for me to shake, her firm grip startled me.

'Welcome to St Bride's, Gemma.' Behind glossy, ruby lips lurked perfect white teeth. 'I'm Oriana Bliss, one of the housemistresses, and you're affiliated to my house. I'm to show you to your flat. Congratulations on your appointment, by the way. A good English teacher is hard to find these days.'

Which is why they'd ended up with me. I wondered how long it would take Oriana and her colleagues to realise I'd never put my teaching qualification into practice.

'Thank you.' My voice was barely audible in this vast space. 'Thank you,' I said again, in case she hadn't heard. This time, my voice rebounded from somewhere near the cherubs. I coughed. 'I was thrilled when Miss Harnett phoned to offer me the job. I thought you would have had much better candidates than me to work at such a beautiful school.' I waved a hand about me, still overwhelmed by the setting. 'Candidates with better qualifications.'

Oriana closed her perfectly made-up eyes, showing off symmetrical half-moons of thick black eyeliner. She let out a chirrup of caustic laughter.

'Good heavens, we're not qualifications snobs here.' She stooped to pick up the smallest of the three bags clustered at my feet. 'Old Hairnet won't even have checked your references if she liked the look of you. Nor will she, so long as you behave yourself.'

I have always been very good at behaving myself. It's the closest thing I have to a superpower.

'Follow me and I'll show you to your flat.'

She swivelled on one stiletto then paced briskly back to the marble staircase. I staggered after her, a suitcase in one hand and my backpack in the other, leaving me with no means of gripping the handrail. I had visions of tumbling awkwardly down the stairs, breaking my neck before I'd had a chance to teach my first lesson. What a shame if I died before even setting foot in my new flat.

Oriana cast her free hand about her, issuing directions.

'Down there's the staff dining room, although from tomorrow we'll be hosting tables in the Trough.'

'The Trough?'

'The girls' dining room. The passage beyond leads to the classroom quad, where the English classroom awaits your personal touch. But that can wait. Let's get you settled into your flat first.'

My flat. Not our flat. Mine. My bags felt lighter.

'You'll be in the Poorhouse.'

'What?'

I'd been expecting to feel like a poor relation amongst the children of the super-rich, but not to be publicly stigmatised.

'That's what the girls call our house. As you'll doubtless have read in the prospectus, for ease of management the school is divided into four boarding houses. Each is named after a saint. The girls have added their own moniker, inspired by the house saint's chief attribute. Ours is St Clare's, as in the Poor Clares, so we're the Poorhouse. The others are Lost and Found (for St Anthony, patron saint of lost causes), the Doghouse (for St Francis, obviously) and the Outhouse (for St Vincent, patron saint of plumbers). The staff in St Vincent are thankful that their nickname is not any worse.'

She gave a wry smile.

'I suppose swearing is against school rules,' I said, smiling back.

'You're right. It doesn't stop them though. The girls swear in code instead. They think the staff haven't rumbled it, but there's a key to the code in the alternative prospectus secretly published by the sixth formers. We've had a copy in the staffroom for years.'

She led me around a corner to a long, dark corridor. 'Rather cleverly, they've devised a system based on quaint expletives culled from school stories of yesteryear. 'Blinking', 'cripes', 'flipping' and so on sound innocuous until you discover they're all paired with alliterative equivalents in the modern vernacular. When they say 'blinking', they're thinking 'bloody'. We turn a deaf ear to them calling each other a 'flipping beast' or whatever, until they slip up, double-compensating, and say the real swear words by mistake. The other girls are genuinely shocked when that happens, and of course we staff have to pretend to be terribly cross.'

'So the girls are generally well behaved?'

She nodded. 'Oh, they're no trouble most of the time. We're pretty strict about most things – no smoking, for example – but we also have some stringent rules on minor issues, such as how to tie their school ties. Breaking those rules satisfies their teenage need to rebel without escalating their misdemeanours to more serious crimes.'

'I suppose the staff aren't allowed to smoke either?'

She stopped sharply, with her back to me. 'Are you a smoker, Gemma?'

'No, never. Not even as a teenager.'

'Then they aren't.'

I thought if I'd said yes, she would have confessed to being a smoker herself.

She halted by an ancient oak door. A large leather fob had been left in the lock. Pulling the brass doorknob towards her, she turned the key clockwise. 'Here you are. You're in Lavender Flat.'

That seemed a good omen. Lavender was my favourite colour.

'The girls call it the Lavatory,' Oriana continued, 'but it's not as bad as that makes it sound.'

I braced myself for the worst that might lie within. Water running down the walls? A foul smell? Graffiti?

Oriana gave the door a firm shove, and it creaked open to reveal my new home. She stood back to allow me to enter first.

To my surprise I found myself in a light, airy space with a bay of huge sash windows. The thick, mauve, brocade curtains complemented the purple Persian rugs scattered carelessly on the gleaming parquet floor.

'Fifty shades of lavender,' said Oriana, whisking dustsheets from the array of antique furniture.

Each piece had clearly been constructed by a master craftsman rather than an amateur with an Allen key, a welcome change from Steven's IKEA collection. The headboard of the high, wide bed was festooned with carvings of ivy and matched a mirror-fronted wardrobe of Narnian proportions. A high-backed sofa upholstered in imperial purple velvet was paired with a generously proportioned footstool, wide enough for three pairs of feet. A magnificent roll-topped bureau supported enough shelves to accommodate many more books than I had brought with me. On the desktop in an antique wooden stationery rack nestled notepaper bearing the school's crest. Picture postcards of the house and grounds reminded me of my parents' collection of National Trust jigsaw puzzles.

I certainly wouldn't be sending a postcard to Steven. I wanted to keep my whereabouts a secret from him, at least until he'd had time to come to terms with the farewell note I'd left for him, to find on his return from his business trip abroad. But I could write a postcard to my parents to tell them my new address, something they'd be relieved to have.

In the wall opposite the window, a tall, marble fireplace housed a cast-iron fire basket stuffed full of pinecones, presumably gathered from the grounds. They might have served as decoration now but would come in handy for kindling as the autumn progressed. I hoped the chimney still worked.

As I gazed about, speechless, Oriana folded the dustsheets and placed them inside an antique oak chest that served as a window seat.

'Hang on to these dustsheets, Gemma, just in case the bursar comes calling,' she was saying. 'Then use them to cover up the decent furniture so he doesn't get any notion of selling it. This bed and wardrobe would fetch a fortune on the antiques market. He's got a bad habit of selling the family silver when he can't make ends meet in the school budget.'

'Goodness.'

'I know, he's infuriating. If he spent less time prowling about the place looking for things to flog and more time at his desk, he could easily solve the shortfall in fees with a little creative accounting.'

'How do you mean?'

'Oh, there are ways he can extract more money from the parents of existing pupils without even putting up the fees.' She waved her hand dismissively as if this were something any fool could do. 'He could slip all kinds of extras under the parents' radar if he tried. He's done it before, like when he started charging all the girls for an annual eye test. While it's only a small amount per girl, it adds up when you're charging for a hundred of them. Of course, they're all eligible for a free eye test on the NHS while they're under eighteen and in full-time education. Most parents have no idea that they're being conned. But my conscience is clear on this, because it saves them the bother of taking their daughters to the optician in the school holidays, so I reckon it's good value for them and they ought to be grateful.'

Perhaps I might have seen it that way too if I were one of the parents: cash-rich and time-poor. Oriana went on.

'He also needs to get his act together on pupil recruitment.'

'Doesn't Miss Harnett do that?'

'She persuades parents that this is the right school for their little darlings when they visit, but the bursar has to lure them here in the first place, and he is spectacularly bad at it. The school can't survive long with just the hundred girls we have now. Even a dozen more girls would make a significant difference. For example, it might enable us to employ a dedicated admissions officer to swell our numbers. And have the full English for breakfast every day instead of eggs and beans.'

My stomach rumbled. I could relate to that argument.

'So if the bursar comes knocking on your door, it's best not to answer. He's not meant to, anyway, other than in an emergency. It's a school rule that staff keep out of each other's flats, for the sake of privacy. It's hard to find any personal space here beyond your flat, so we respect it as a boundary. And whatever you do, don't invite any of the governors into your bed.'

My eyes widened in horror. 'That idea had not entered my head.'

Oriana shrugged. 'Nonetheless, I always warn newbies against it after what happened to poor Caroline.'

Before she could explain, an old-fashioned dinner gong sounded in the distance, and she held up her hand to cut our conversation short. 'Lunchtime. You can't hang about at mealtimes in this place or you'll starve. We'd better leg it.'

Hoping her swivelling stilettos wouldn't bore a hole in my beautiful old rug, I followed her out of the room, wondering just what had happened to 'poor Caroline'.

2

TABLE MANNERS

After fleeting introductions around the table to my new colleagues, none of whom were called Caroline, Oriana pointed to a free place at the near side of the dining table. I was quickly to learn that here, and in the staffroom, every teacher had a designated seat. The longest-serving staff had the best ones, and you broke the pecking order at your peril.

'After lunch, someone will give you the full tour,' said Oriana, once we'd started tucking into the excellent shepherd's pie laid out in vast serving dishes along the table. 'Then you'll have the rest of the afternoon to settle into your flat and unpack before the girls arrive.'

'Thank you, but I've already had a tour of the school. The bursar showed me the staffroom and the classrooms when I came for my interview.'

The flashing of cutlery came to a halt as the assembled staff exchanged knowing looks.

'Then you have seen only a tiny part,' Nicolette Renoir,

sitting opposite me, said with a soft French accent. 'You must see the rest.'

'Are you volunteering, Nicolette?' Oriana said, laying her knife and fork neatly across her empty plate and dabbing the corners of her mouth with a pristine linen napkin. Somehow she'd managed to clear her plate without disturbing her lipstick. I wondered whether she'd had her lips tattooed.

Nicolette shook her head. 'Ask Joscelyn to take her. *Vive la liberté*. I want to be alone until the flipping beasts return.' I was impressed at the French teacher's grasp of vintage vernacular until I remembered the girls' secret code.

She turned to me. 'Please do not think I am being unhelpful, Miss Lamb, but like Miss Bliss I am also a housemistress. Once the girls arrive, I will not have a moment of peace until half term.' She reached across to pat my hand as she flashed an agreeable and genuine smile. 'But do not worry, *ma chérie*, I will be there for you if you need me.'

'She will, too,' said a cheerful voice behind me – unmistakably the voice of a man. What on earth was a man doing here? The prospectus had made it very clear St Bride's employed only female staff. That was part of its appeal to me, as well as to prospective pupils' parents.

'You should know, you old goat,' said Mavis Brook, the geography teacher, who looked well beyond retirement age. Her tousled appearance gave the impression that she had spent the day outdoors observing a powerful storm. Her hair must once have been auburn. Now diluted with white, it was turning from flame to ash.

The source of Mavis's scorn pulled out the remaining empty chair, immediately to my right. Judging by the 'old goat' comment, I had expected the subject of her remark to be of a similar age to herself, so was startled to find my shoulder being patted by a firm-fleshed hand with broad, sturdy fingers as an athletic thirty-something settled in beside me.

'Hello, you,' he beamed, assuming a level of intimacy that I wasn't expecting.

All eyes around the table switched from him to me to gauge my reaction. I proceeded with caution.

'Hello, er…'

'Joe. I'm Joe.' His friendly smile was all wide-eyed inno-cence, his eyes the deepest blue. 'The PE teacher.'

'Hello, Joe,' I said slowly. 'Are you also new here this term?' The staff seemed surprisingly familiar with him if he'd only just arrived. 'I don't remember noticing any male staff in the prospectus. And the only staff mentioned, apart from the bursar, were either Mrs, Miss, or Ms.'

'Yes, that's right. Miss J. Spryke. The J's for Joscelyn – but everyone calls me Joe these days.'

Before I could stop myself, I flashed a look at his chin. His shoulder-length wavy hair was as golden as the newly harvested cornfields that bordered the St Bride's estate, but, unlike the fields, his chin was stubble-free.

'Oh, I see.' I felt everyone's eyes upon me. 'So you finished last term as Joscelyn, and you've come back as Joe. I get it now. Sorry to be so dense. I didn't realise one could transition so quickly.'

A ripple of laughter – kindly laughter, but at me, not with me – ran around the table. I hoped I hadn't put my foot in it.

Joe patted my hand. 'Don't mind them, sweetheart. You've just proven to us yet again that the head's strategy works.'

'Miss Hairnet's strategy?' I blurted. I wished Oriana hadn't told me the headmistress's nickname. I'd be forever nervous now of accidentally saying it to her face.

Joe reached across to the nearest food warmer, on which the remains of a shepherd's pie was crisping at the edges. He offered it to me and I took a modest amount, having already cleared my plate once, then he helped himself to a distinctly 'man-sized' portion. Apart from Oriana, the rest of the staff looked as if they enjoyed school food.

'School marketing strategy, signed off by the governors, in their wisdom.' He slid a forkful of mash enthusiastically into his mouth. When he swallowed, a very noticeable Adam's apple bobbed up and down. 'No mention is to be made of male staff anywhere in school marketing materials – website, prospectus, social media – or anywhere else. The suggestion of an all-female staff encourages the more protective parents – our target market – to entrust their precious daughters into our tender care. Therefore only female staff are pictured in the prospectus.'

I thought for a moment. 'Apart from being overprotective, isn't it sexist to assume that only men could corrupt or abuse children?'

'Positively Victorian,' said Judith Gosling, the history teacher, tucking into a second helping of shepherd's pie.

'Fathers believe what they want to believe about their daughters,' said Louisa Humber, Head of Music. 'I'm not surprised so many are taken in.'

I frowned. 'What about the mothers?'

'We have an unusually high proportion of pupils here who are motherless,' said Felicity Button, head of life skills. 'All of them, in fact. That was one of Lord Bunting's founding principles, established in his will. Motherless pupils receive a significant discount. He wanted the school to act *in loco maternis*.'

'What about fatherless girls?' It seemed an odd bias.

Joe shrugged. 'He didn't seem so bothered about those, for some reason. Still, that's not all bad news, is it, Oriana?' The corners of Joe's mouth twitched. 'All the more widowed fathers for you to choose from.'

So that was why she was so smartly dressed: to greet the imminent arrival of a bevy of rich widowers.

'I don't know what you mean,' Oriana said coolly.

'Doesn't that make the prospectus misleading?' I didn't want to offend anyone, but nor was I willing to be party to fraud.

Hazel Taylor, head of art, passed Joe the water jug and he topped up my glass before filling his own.

'Not really. There's no deception. I'm within my rights to request that my picture doesn't appear in the prospectus, or in any other school publicity material. Same goes for the girls. I'm a private person.'

'We don't need to know what you get up to in private.' Mavis again. 'Prig.'

He didn't seem remotely priggish to me, then I realised she was using the girls' code.

'But surely parents must meet you in person some time? Or spot you on the sports field during matches?'

Joe was unfazed. 'No problem if they do. They expect the PE teacher in a girls' school to look a bit rugged.' When he slapped his thigh proudly, I noticed for the first time that he was wearing a white tennis skirt.

'Oh, and the girls call him "Miss",' said Dr Teresa Fleming, the head of science, a dark-haired lady in round gold glasses and a white lab coat. 'That helps.'

The other teachers had cleared and removed their plates and were tucking into a blood-red cherry pie. I wondered which one was Caroline, but didn't like to ask, in case anyone wanted to know my reason for enquiring. Nor did I want to immediately associate myself with someone in disgrace.

Then it occurred to me: perhaps Caroline was no longer even employed at the school. Had her misdemeanour led to her dismissal? If so, it was important I should find out what it was so that I could avoid making the same mistake myself. I didn't want anything to threaten my position here.

Snapping out of my reverie, I realised I was way behind my colleagues with my meal. I resumed eating my main course in the hope of catching up. I didn't want to miss out on that luscious pudding.

I still couldn't believe such an obvious deception could work so I turned back to Joe. 'Don't the girls talk to their parents about you? Aren't you worried about them giving the game away?'

Nicolette answered on Joe's behalf. 'Most of our girls are teenagers. *Regarde le, ma chérie.* If you were fifteen, would you exchange him for a woman?'

Seeing her point, I tried to broaden the conversation. 'So, are there any other male staff here or are you the only one?'

'There's Max, the security guard,' said Oriana, who had already finished her cherry pie. She set down her napkin. 'Of course, Max is not his real name. Doting fathers are simply assured that 'maximum security is provided for the girls' safety'. That's where his nickname comes from. His main role is to patrol the grounds outside of teaching hours and through the night, so you won't usually see much of him. But I expect you'll meet him at some point today, as he works days on the first and last day of term.'

'Then there's the housekeeper, Gerry Brompton,' added Joe, scraping his spoon around his bowl to capture every last drop of cherry juice. 'All the girls call him Gerry. If they ever mention Gerry at home, the fathers will assume he's a woman. But Gerry's short for Gerald, not Geraldine. He's an experienced hotelier and we're lucky to have him.'

'Buzzards?'

Oriana raised a slender forefinger. 'Remind me to find you a copy of the alternative prospectus, Gemma.'

'But surely parents must realise you're a man when they come to parents' evenings?'

Joe set his knife and fork down together on his empty plate and patted his taut tummy in appreciation.

'On parents' evenings I raise my voice an octave and keep my distance, so no one rumbles my disguise. If any have their doubts about me, they are too polite to say openly, and their daughters will cover for me – those that realise. A lot of the little ones think I'm a woman too.'

It all seemed a bit odd. Even if there was no real harm done – and I wanted to assume there wasn't, as I was starting to like it here and had nowhere else to go – it must be a tricky act to sustain.

'But what about inter-school matches? Don't parents ever watch their daughters play competitive sport against other schools? Or against each other on Sports Day?'

Joe shook his head. 'Out of respect for the wishes of our more sensitive parents, who happen also to be our biggest benefactors, we do not stage any events that allow our pupils to "parade themselves in public in their underwear", as Mr Khan put it. For which most of the other parents are mightily relieved. They've got much better things to do than spend their leisure hours standing on the touchline. By the way, I'll show you the new Khan Olympic Swimming Pool later.'

As Oriana glanced at the gold watch that embraced her slender wrist, I noticed her impeccable French manicure. Her innate elegance made her stand out among her colleagues. I wondered whether she had been a pupil here herself and had a private income supplementing her teacher's salary.

'Speaking of leisure hours, we've just got time for coffee in the staffroom before we take up our welcoming posts in the hall. The little beasts will start arriving back any minute. Joe, in the meantime, take Gemma on the staff tour, will you?'

'Sure,' said Joe. He turned to me. 'I keep a low profile on drop-off and pick-up days, for obvious reasons.'

As the others headed off to the staffroom, a wide-eyed, grey-haired lady in a white housecoat entered the room and began gathering everyone's empty dessert bowls and spoons. She stacked them on a large aluminium trolley presumably destined for the dishwasher. I scooped up my last forkful of shepherd's pie.

'Wonderful lunch, as ever, Rosemary,' said Joe.

His gratitude was echoed around the table.

'But Gemma, before I show you around, let's finish up that cherry pie.'

He grabbed the remains of the last one before Rosemary could remove it.

He cut me a generous helping of pie and slid it on to my plate, then passed me the cream jug, handle towards me. Everyone here had such good table manners, so refreshing after dining with Steven for so long. Though courteous in company, he never felt he had to mind his manners in front of me.

I wondered whether Joe's cute lopsided smile was the result of an injury on the sports field. I looked forward to seeing him in action, wondering what his main sport was.

'You look like you could do with a good square meal or two,' he continued. He was right, too. I'd got into the habit of not eating much when Steven wasn't around. Somehow it had made me feel better. It was about the only area of my life over which I had total control.

'School food's always best at the start of term, by the way, so make the most of it before it fizzles out,' he added.

'Why's that? Is the chef not good at making her budget last?'

Joe grinned. 'That's not the problem. What happens is she gets distracted. Rosemary is married to Max, you see, and during term time they hardly see each other due to their different shifts. She's on days, he's on nights. After a few weeks, it starts getting to her. By the second half of term, her mind's not on her job.'

With an encouraging smile, he helped me to seconds.

He cut himself an even larger, second slice of pie and drenched the crisp lattice pastry top with cream. Realising I was watching him, he gave me an encouraging smile.

'Don't mind me, Gemma, I fill my boots at school meal-times. Not like Oriana. She starves herself during the school holidays to look sylphlike for the fathers at the start of term, then eats like a horse until a few weeks before we break up.'

I wondered whether he was carb-loading for some energetic activity that afternoon.

'Just remember,' he added. 'What happens on the new teacher's tour stays on the new teacher's tour.'

I paused with my loaded spoon over my bowl, a succulent cherry oozing juice from where I'd pierced it with my fork.

'You're not by any chance a school governor, are you?'

It was Joe's turn to look startled. 'No, of course not. Why do you ask?'

'No reason.' I returned my attention to my pie, wondering whether or not to be pleased.

3

DRESSING DOWN

'You're probably the wrong person to ask whether there's a staff dress code, but I'll ask you anyway.'

More at ease with Joe in his sports kit than with the elegant Oriana, I wished I'd taken more notice of what the other teachers had been wearing. I wanted to make a good first impression on my pupils.

As we strolled out of the classroom quad, Joe cast a glance at my tailored trousers and blouse.

'You look fine to me. Sorry, I forget how much easier it is for me than for the rest of the staff. My role and my timetable define my outfit down to the last detail. Mind you, I wouldn't mind being a science teacher. Dr Fleming can wear anything at all beneath the statutory lab coat. Or indeed nothing at all. That must be liberating.'

I wondered whether he'd discovered that first-hand.

'So I won't be out of place if I'm not dressed up in smart skirts and high heels like Oriana?'

'Not at all. She won't be like that tomorrow anyway, not

once all the rich dads are off the scene. That's just her recruiting outfit.'

'I didn't know she was involved in staff recruitment? She didn't interview me.'

'Recruiting for a husband, I mean. A rich widower to whisk her away from all this. But don't worry, there's no unbreakable dress code. Just don't wear anything that would frighten the horses in the streets or shock any visiting grandmothers. That's what all the other staff do.'

That was a relief.

'So have I met all the other teachers now?' I asked, trying to steer the conversation around to the elusive Caroline. 'Were they all at lunch with us?'

Joe nodded and reeled off the list of names, which didn't include a Caroline, or any diminutive of Caroline. It seemed whatever Caroline had done had got her fired. I really needed to find out what that was, so I could avoid making the same mistake.

'Don't worry if you can't remember all their names for now. Oh, and when we're with the girls, we don't address each other by our Christian names. It helps maintain our authority.'

I gazed across the immaculate terraced lawns to the grazing pastures beyond. 'There are a lot of horses round here, aren't there? Though not many streets.'

'Nor many grandmothers. Or people in general. For the girls' parents, the remote rural location is a big part of the school's charm, especially for those whose daughters are at significant risk of kidnap.'

I stopped and stared at him. 'Really? We've got pupils who might get kidnapped?'

He nodded and walked on, and I ran a couple of steps to catch up. 'Oh yes, that's why Hairnet employs Max, our security officer, to keep them all out of harm's way.'

That was reassuring. If a security officer was ensuring the school was safe for the pupils, the teachers must also fall under his protection. Not that I thought Steven would kidnap me, but just the thought of him discovering my hideaway and coming to find me made me feel sick. Even with fifty miles between us, I was still afraid of him.

'You see, we've plenty of millionaires' daughters,' Joe was explaining. 'Heiresses to household brand names or large property portfolios. Some girls have titles. Not that we use those in school, of course.'

'Why, is it run on republican principles?'

'Oh no. The headmistress loves a good royal. In the presence of a title, she's got an infallible curtsey reflex. She just doesn't want the untitled girls sucking up to the titled ones, assuming they're loaded. Often they're skint. Well, relatively, anyway. Not many of our pupils are what you'd call poor.'

'Really? I'd heard that at the best boarding schools, there's a real social mix – not just rich kids, but children with working-class parents who scrimp and save and work extra jobs to give them all the advantages of a private education. I gather there are subsidies for motherless students here, which must be an extra draw for less affluent parents, on top of the smarter facilities, smaller classes, better exam results—'

'Better teachers. Like you and me.' That mischievous smile again.

I feigned humility, or rather, I feigned the need to feign humility. Meanwhile I was beginning to realise how irresponsible I'd been to take this job. With my lack of teaching experience since I'd completed my training, I might have singlehandedly triggered a downward trajectory in the school's English exam results the following summer.

I was glad when Joe went off on a different tangent.

'It's not like that at St Bride's. Miss Harnett's too thoughtful to let any family near-bankrupt themselves to pay our school fees. Instead she lets a few in for free on the sly, only breaking it to the bursar afterwards once the deal is signed and sealed. It's good to have them on board, despite the strain they put on the school's budget. They're a good counterbalance to the TFB, who are just biding their time till they get their financial independence.'

'TFB?'

'Trust Fund Brigade. But don't get too hung up about the politics. For the staff it's a good life once you get into the swing of it, and the girls are happy enough. We take good care of them, and in the scheme of things, their parents get good value for money. So just relax and enjoy the ride.'

Taking me firmly by the hand, he led me off the gravel path and into a tangle of waist-high weeds down a steeply sloping bank. He trampled down nettles and brambles to clear the way for me without a thought for his bare calves, and we were soon out of sight of the school building.

4

MAXIMUM SECURITY

'The name's Security, Max Security.'

A pale, wiry figure of uncertain age emerged at our feet from beneath a leaf-covered camouflage net. 'Well, actually it's not,' he continued, 'but if I told you my real name, I'd have to kill you.'

I hoped his deadpan manner indicated dry humour rather than murderous intent.

As he threw back the net and stood up, I realised he'd just climbed out of a hole in the ground. Not a rabbit hole, like *Alice in Wonderland*'s, but a square structure, reinforced with bricks and concrete, with a metal ladder embedded in its side. If there'd been a house on top of it, I'd have called it a storm cellar. I wondered whether it led to an underground bunker.

Max drew himself up to his full height, towering over Joe as well as me. Then he dragged the net up behind him, pulled it over his head, and let it hang down over his whole body, like a camouflaged ghost. He glanced rapidly to the left and right.

'It's okay Max, we're quite alone,' said Joe. 'This is just a flying visit to introduce you formally to our newest member of staff, Gemma Lamb, while the rest of the team welcome the girls.'

'Good call. Gemma needs to get the lie of the land before we let the parents loose on her.' Max appraised me with a long, hard stare, pink-rimmed eyes squinting against the sunshine. With his dark receding hair slicked back from his forehead, he reminded me of a mole.

Uncomfortable under his penetrating gaze, I broke eye contact, only to find myself transfixed by his combat trousers. I'd never seen combat trousers used in anger before. I kept things like my phone and tissues in mine. Max's bulged with handcuffs and batons which peeked out of the pockets.

Joe laid a reassuring hand on my shoulder. 'Don't worry, Gemma. Max is on our side.'

I was glad he thought so.

'So, what's your story, Gemma Lamb?' asked Max. 'Anything I should know about you? What are you running away from? That's what they all do here, you know. They're all on the run from something.'

I let out a strangled laugh and brushed Joe's hand away. 'On the run? What, you mean like criminals?'

Joe slipped his hands into the pockets of his tennis skirt. 'What Max means is that staff come here for a fresh start. Just like the girls.'

Max nodded. 'Joe here wanted to start over after the premature end of his career as a professional athlete.'

Joe certainly had the build of a career athlete. I wondered what kind of injury had curtailed his success. He wasn't limping.

'Which was your sport, Joe?' I asked.

Should I have heard of him? Not that I could have named many famous sportspeople, despite Steven's addiction to Sky Sports. He wasn't Mo Farah nor Andy Murray, I knew that much.

'Cycling.' Joe sounded less enthusiastic than I'd expected. 'But no sportsperson's career lasts long these days. I haven't cycled competitively for ages. Now I just see a bike as a form of transport, and the only reason I cycle anywhere is because I don't have a car.'

Max leaned towards me. 'But when he does get on a bike, you should see him go! Dashes down that drive in a blur.'

'Well, the drive is nearly a mile long,' said Joe. 'There's plenty of time to get a good speed up.'

Max nodded. 'Goes like a rocket, he does. If there was a superhero called Cycleman who cycled at the speed of light, Joe here would be his daytime persona.'

Joe shuffled his trainers in the scrubby grass.

'Yes, well, enough about me and my illustrious past. This tour's about Gemma, not me. Gemma, anything you need to tell Max?'

'I didn't learn to ride a bike till I was twelve.'

'I mean in his professional capacity. Any security worries? I can leave you alone with him to discuss it if that helps.'

When Joe took a step back, as if about to depart, I grabbed his arm quickly. I wasn't sure I wanted to be alone with this coiled spring in fully-loaded combat trousers.

For a moment, I wondered whether I should mention my fear of Steven, but decided against it. It wasn't as if he even knew where I was, so it hardly counted as a threat. Besides, I was ashamed of my failed relationship and I didn't want to seem weak or vulnerable in front of my new colleagues. This job was meant to be a fresh start and I wanted to leave my baggage behind me. I decided to make light of the question instead.

'That won't be necessary, thanks. I've nothing to declare. No secret stash of gold bullion beneath my bed, if that's the sort of thing you mean.'

I forced a laugh, but Max's face was serious.

'Gold bullion wouldn't be such an issue, as it's very heavy to carry off. Cash, now, that's more of a temptation. Much easier to steal, and more tempting in low denominations. Big notes are harder to spend.'

Joe glanced at his chunky sports watch. On a less muscular arm it would have looked ungainly. 'I guess we're all done here, Gemma. We should press on and leave Max to carry out his surveillance duties once the girls start arriving.' He turned to Max. 'Good to see you, Max. Perhaps we'll catch up on my afternoon off for a game of poker?'

Max grinned for the first time. 'Always happy to take your money, son.' Then he startled me by standing to attention and offering a brisk military salute. 'Pleasure to meet you too, ma'am.'

The only salute I was qualified to do was the one I'd used to make my Brownie Promise. I couldn't remember which fingers to use, so I simply smiled politely and said goodbye. Immediately, Max threw his camouflage net down the hole in the ground and clambered after it, his steel toe-caps dinging against the metal ladder. Once his head was below ground level, he reached up to pull the turf-covered hatch back into place – a metal drain cover, disguised with fake grass. I watched Joe's muscular calf flex as he trod down the real grass that had been disturbed at the edge of the hatch until we couldn't see the join. The uninitiated would never have guessed what lay beneath.

I frowned, puzzled.

'How can Max keep a lookout for the girls from down there?'

Joe beckoned me back up the slope, offering me his hand to haul me up to the main path. I hesitated. He seemed to be touching me a lot for someone I'd only just met. But the bank was steep, so I accepted.

'Oh, he doesn't. That's just an entry point to one of the underground tunnels. He'll be off to the hatch by the cattle grid on the drive now, to watch the comings and goings of the girls and their parents, counting them in and out, logging car registration plates and so on.'

'You mean he pops up like a meerkat at strategic points around the school? I can picture him springing out of grassy knolls like a Teletubby.'

Joe narrowed his eyes. 'A meerkat whose hands are registered with the police as a deadly weapon. A Teletubby who keeps knuckledusters in his big red handbag. That's Max's story, anyway.'

5

THE LOVE OF MONEY

We returned to the open, sweeping lawn that ran around the back of the main school building. The grass was so neat that I wondered for a moment whether it was artificial. Then I realised it was the kind of lawn you get if you roll it regularly for a couple of hundred years – the sort of lawn my father aspires to have. I wondered how my parents' garden was looking these days. I missed it.

I longed to kick my shoes off and feel the cool blades of grass tickling the soles of my feet – something I hadn't done for ages. I used to do it at home in my parents' garden all the time. Steven's flat didn't have a garden, and besides he didn't like me taking off my shoes in public. Remembering this had me wondering whether the school's gardening staff were male or female. There must be a hidden army of them to keep the place so immaculate.

We began to walk around the neat circuit of paths, crisp golden gravel crunching agreeably beneath our feet. Just as well I'd kept my shoes on after all.

My thoughts went back to Max.

'How did you know Max was going to be there then to introduce me?'

Joe shrugged. 'It's where he generally hangs out at the start of term, checking his radar before the girls arrive.'

Before I could ask whether the radar was real or metaphorical, Joe went on to sing Max's praises.

'That's what you want in a good security man, though, isn't it? Anticipation? Initiative? The element of surprise? You can never be quite sure where he will turn up next.'

'Not so much the Scarlet Pimpernel, more the Camouflage Carnation.'

Joe grinned. 'You academics, you're way ahead of me.'

We turned a corner to take a path that ran along the furthest edge of the lawns, gaining a spectacular view of the mansion.

'So how come there's a hole in the ground there? Did he dig it out himself?'

Joe laughed. 'He's tough, but not that tough. No, it was created by Lord Bunting, who built the house.'

'That's a funny hobby for a member of the gentry. I wouldn't have thought he'd have wanted to get his hands dirty like that.'

'Well, when I say by him, I mean under his direction. Bunting was an engineer and invented a highly efficient means of digging tunnels. In the age of the railway and the London Underground, it made him a fortune. It was also used extensively for building drains. That's why one of the school's houses is named after the patron saint of plumbers, in memory of Bunting's achievements.'

A growing breeze rustled the vast chestnut tree ahead of us, and I wished I'd brought a jacket.

'So he used it to dig Max's bunker?'

'More than that. He dug a whole network of tunnels beneath his estate.'

'He built his own private underground railway beneath the school? Goodness!'

I looked down at my feet, listening for tell-tale noises of engines.

'No, silly, just tunnels, for their own sake, but based on the same model as his railway tunnels. I don't know why he wanted to fillet his estate like that. Some say it was to demonstrate his patented equipment to visitors, others to give shelter to estate workers caught out on the land in foul weather. I reckon he just wanted to play with his toy. Anyway, the tunnels were invaluable as air raid shelters during the Second World War, and now they come in handy for Max's surveillance purposes. They're a useful resource in addition to his network of hidden cameras, so no one's complaining.'

What about our human rights? I wanted to ask, wondering where the cameras were hidden. But I didn't want to draw attention to how uncomfortable the idea of surveillance made me in case Joe thought I had something to hide. I wondered whether Max's cameras were also inside the building. Surely the pupils' parents wouldn't want a strange man ogling their daughters unawares?

We turned right again and passed through the lychgate into the small walled churchyard surrounding what I took to be the school chapel. Joe turned the brass handle on the porch door and held it open for me to enter. It was mostly dark inside, but instead of containing an altar and pews, there was just a pair of raised tombs facing each other beneath arched stained-glass windows. I realised it wasn't a chapel at all, but some kind of mausoleum.

'Here's another glimpse into Lord Bunting's world.' He pointed to a creamy statue of a bearded gentleman reclining on his elbow on top of the left-hand tomb. I half-expected Max to lift its lid and pop up again like a military jack-in-the-box, until I realised just how heavy such a large slab of marble would be.

I approached the statue and patted Lord Bunting's ice-cold hand. 'What an extraordinary man.'

For a moment, we stood gazing in admiration, and I realised that without this man's achievements in Victorian times, I'd never have come to this place, or met Oriana, or Joe, or Max, or had this chance for a fresh start.

I looked across to the other tomb, wondering why there was no matching statue of his wife.

'Where's Lady Bunting? I take it there was one.'

Joe gave a sympathetic smile. 'Oh yes, there was a Lady Bunting all right. The poor old boy had always fondly assumed she'd be with him in death as in life, hence the second plinth. But he hadn't counted on her getting a better offer from another even wealthier gentleman when he predeceased her. She went on to have a second long and happy marriage, and now her old bones rest in a fancier setting on another man's family estate.'

'I'm surprised she wasn't tempted to bring him to live here.'

'She couldn't. She forfeited Lord Bunting's estate on her remarriage.'

'That must have pleased the next in line.'

Joe shook his head. 'There wasn't one. Bunting entailed the estate such that when his wife either died or remarried, the whole place should be turned into an educational charity for girls. And here we are.'

'Lady Bunting must have loved her second husband a great deal to be prepared to give all this up.'

'Either him or his estate,' said Joe. 'Now, we'd better put on a spurt. I've just got time to show you the kitchen garden. It's completely out of bounds to the girls, so a useful outdoor escape for the staff. And on the way there, you can tell me what you didn't seem to want to tell Max – what brought you to St Bride's in the first place. Because one thing's for sure: it wasn't the salary.'

'Salary?' As we crossed the lawn, I played for time by making a joke. 'You mean we get paid as well? Bed and board in this beautiful place will be quite enough for me.'

We passed through a dark oak doorway to enter the old walled garden. The rosy-red bricks on all four sides were complemented by neat rows of creamy leeks, tightly furled cabbages, golden onions, and green beans. In the far corner stood an ancient wrought-iron greenhouse painted white, with scarlet tomatoes and golden peppers glinting in the sun behind its warming glass.

Joe was not so easily diverted. 'I know you must be running away from something.'

I thought fast. 'Why shouldn't I be running towards something, rather than away from it? Towards a brand-new teaching career?'

'Aha, so you admit you've never actually taught before?'

I put my hands over my mouth too late to stop my indiscretion, and he grinned.

'Don't worry, I hadn't either.'

'But I am a trained teacher,' I said quickly. 'I did well in my teaching practice placements. And I've got a good English degree from a decent university.'

'Oh, you'll do, I'm sure.' He waved a hand dismissively. 'Don't worry, I'm only teasing you. But how come, if you did all that training, you've never taught till now? Surely you must have wanted to?'

I hesitated, wondering whether I could trust him enough to tell him that Steven didn't want me to teach. Steven claimed he didn't want us to have to take our holidays outside of term time, but I knew there was more to it than that. He was very possessive and would have been jealous of me mixing with so many other adults, particularly men. I remained silent.

'Okay, tell me some other time, then. But take heart, Gemma. Whatever you're fleeing, you've chosen a good bolt-hole. St Bride's is a safe little bubble, protected from reality, and not only by Max's efforts. It's the Cotswolds' answer to Shangri-La, offering us a standard of living that not even a teacher at the top of the salary scale could ever have the chance to enjoy. Peace and quiet, fresh air and tranquillity, excellent food in generous helpings—'

'Our own flats,' I added with feeling. 'It all sounds too good to be true.'

'It's not perfect, though. We do lack privacy. Staff can get a bit on top of each other. Sometimes it's hard to find space to be alone.'

'I thought the staff seemed pretty sociable at lunchtime.'

'Only because they hadn't seen each other for the last two months. But you're right, they don't want solitude all the time, and I'm sure you don't either.'

As we passed the herb beds, I bent to pluck a sprig of rosemary, crushing it to release its astringent smell and holding it to my nose. My dad always used to grow rosemary.

'Speaking of running away, don't the girls ever try to make a bid for freedom? I mean, I can see how for jaded adults this place might seem like a sanctuary, but for the average teenager, it must be a nightmare.'

'Max's job is as much to keep the girls in as to keep intruders out. We give them a full timetable and take registers at every lesson. Fortunately, they're mostly gullible enough to be afraid of ghosts, so Max makes the odd patrol above ground in his phosphorescent suit a couple of times a term, and that's enough to deter them from making a run for it under cover of night.'

We passed back through the garden door set in the brickwork and headed back to the house. As we got closer, we could hear the hum of cars coming down the drive, and the high-pitched chatter of excitable girls reunited with their friends after the long summer holidays.

'Anyway, just trust me. Tell me your secrets, and I'll look out for you as much as Max does.'

I was bursting to tell someone about leaving Steven, but could I trust a man I'd only just met? I wasn't sure I even trusted myself yet. Some things are best kept secret.

I pulled the cuffs of my blouse down over my wrists. The bruises from my most recent row with Steven had almost faded. Not only our most recent, but our last, I hoped, for ever. Provided I didn't go back.

'You first,' I said quickly. 'Tell me what you were running from.'

'Cycling,' he said. 'I'm Cycleman, remember?'

Just then the school bell rang, marking the deadline for the girls' return to school.

'Saved by the bicycle bell,' I joked lamely, thankful to cut the conversation short before he could grill me any further.

6

WAKE-UP CALL

The hammering at the door to my flat the next morning was so loud that, for a moment, I wondered whether one of the governors Oriana had warned me about had come to claim *droit de seigneur*. A high-pitched voice put my mind at rest.

'Miss Lamb, Miss Lamb, it's Imogen, come to take you to breakfast.'

I hauled the door open to find a small girl with a white-blonde ponytail and an immaculate school uniform.

It was my first sight of the St Bride's attire outside of the prospectus, my interview having taken place in the school holidays. The mauve tartan kilt, nearly reaching her black-socked ankles and brogues, was smart and timeless. Expensive, too, judging by how well the fine wool pleats hung. The navy tie knotted over her crisp white shirt bore a gilt-edged prefect's badge, although she couldn't have been more than twelve. What a remarkable child she must be to have been made prefect already – a future prime minister, perhaps.

'Thank you, Imogen,' I said, fetching my key and locking

the door to my flat behind me. 'I'm glad you've come. I'm not sure I'd remember my way to the staff dining room.'

As I followed her, she stretched out a hand to point which way to turn, like a diminutive traffic cop.

'Oh, we're not going to the staff dining room,' she said cheerfully. 'In term time you get to have your meals in the Trough with us girls.' She spoke as if it were a special treat.

'Of course, Miss Bliss told me. I'm sorry, I'd forgotten.'

'Breakfast together is a lovely way to start the day. We don't get this at home, you know. I never see Daddy till he comes home after work. I like to start the day with a good grown-up chat. We all do.'

She tripped down the marble stairs with Oriana's lightness of foot. Clinging to the banister, I wondered whether this required special training. Mastering this staircase would be the ideal preparation for debutantes' coming-out balls. Most of the pupils probably moved in that kind of social circle.

'And I'm glad I was sent to fetch you, because it means I get to go down the marble stairs. They're out of bounds for girls otherwise.'

For a child whose father could afford the school fees to regard the use of a staircase, no matter how grand, as a wondrous treat seemed odd.

She pointed across the entrance hall and led me to a double door that opened into a high-ceilinged central atrium. In the far corners were two doors exactly alike. The one in the left-hand corner was distinguished by the racket that came from beyond it. It sounded like a riot in full swing. I glanced at Imogen to see whether the noise troubled her. Undaunted, she raised her voice above the hubbub as she swung the door open, before standing back to let me go in first.

'Teachers take the chairs at the ends of the tables. We're on the top table, by the bay window.'

For a moment I stood on the threshold, taking in a sea of a hundred young faces somehow managing to demolish great plates of scrambled eggs and baked beans while chattering at the tops of their voices. Juice jugs rattled against crystal tumblers, silver serving spoons against chafing dishes, while the girls jiggled their chairs about on the gleaming parquet floor.

'Coffee or tea, Miss Lamb?' asked Imogen, closing the door behind us.

'Coffee, please, black, no sugar,' I said, as all the girls turned appraisingly in my direction.

'Don't mind them, little beasts,' said Imogen brightly. 'They're just being nosy because you're new. Go and sit down and I'll fetch your coffee.'

I fixed a smile on my face as I edged down the room towards our table. Girls in my path scraped their chairs closer to their tables to allow me through. It was a relief to reach my appointed table, until all the girls arrayed around it stopped talking, stood up, and fixed me with expectant stares. All nine of them bore the prefect's badge of office, despite being about the same age as Imogen.

Imogen quickly came to my rescue, marching up to set a silver tray with a coffee pot, a china cup and saucer, and a silver spoon by my place. Then she stood on tiptoe to whisper in my ear, 'They won't sit down until you do. It's the law.'

Intensely grateful for her continuing advice, I dared to

hope Imogen might somehow convey to me which rule Caroline had broken, so that I might avoid it. In the meantime, I was glad to be coached through the etiquette of breakfast. The sooner I learned the school rules the better. When Imogen nodded her head towards my chair, I sat down more abruptly than I'd intended. Ten small bottoms plopped down on the chairs around me, and the girls' chatter resumed.

I was glad the chair next to me had been left empty for Imogen.

'I'll give you a rundown of the Trough Rules,' she said. 'No one leaves their table till everybody else on it has finished. But no one should take so long that they hold everyone else up. If you want something like the eggs or the salt, you're not allowed to just take it. You have to offer it to someone else first, then they'll know to offer it to you. You must use your knife and fork or spoon at all times, except for toast, which like everything else you have to cut into bite-sized pieces first. No tearing things apart with your teeth. Same goes for fruit. Especially bananas. I don't know why.'

'Would you like some more eggs, Miss Lamb, and some beans?' asked a girl with short dark curls to my right.

'But I haven't had any yet—'

When Imogen nudged me with her toe under the table, I realised I'd broken the first rule already.

'Oh, I'm sorry, would *you* like some more eggs and beans?'

My young inquisitor beamed. 'Yes please, Miss Lamb, how very kind.' Without further ado, she filled her plate with both and started to tuck in.

'Now your turn,' said Imogen.

'Imogen, would you like some eggs and beans?'

'Yes please, Miss Lamb. How kind. Would you?'

This was starting to feel like a game of Happy Families. Remembering Imogen's sad comment about never seeing her father at breakfast, I wondered whether this was part of Miss Harnett's plan.

I felt I'd earned my meal. The delicious hot coffee bucked me up no end, as did the velvety scrambled egg, redolent of thick cream. (I wasn't going to risk the beans, for fear of social death in the classroom.)

Imogen sensed my shyness. She leaned close to me again. 'Miss Harnett always says, if you can't think of what to say in conversation, ask people questions about themselves, and it'll make them like you more. Everyone likes talking about themselves.'

I wasn't sure I did, but I trusted Imogen's judgement and decided to give it a go.

'You all look very smart,' I began, surveying their neat shirts and ties. 'I expect it feels strange to be back in uniform after the summer holidays.'

A red-headed girl with straight plaits gave an enormous sigh. 'Oh, it's a blinking relief, Miss Lamb. No more worries about what to wear or what other people are wearing. I mean, no one cares what they look like here.'

'Well, I think you all look lovely.'

'So do you, Miss Lamb,' one of them replied. I didn't mind whether or not she was just being polite. It was the first time anyone had told me that for a very long time. I liked these girls already.

I glanced around the dining hall to see which other staff were in attendance. All those I'd met already, plus a few more, were heading up tables. Nicolette caught me looking at her and kissed her fingers to me. I couldn't remember the last time anyone had done that, either, not since my mum used to wave me off to school. I smiled back before I noticed that my table had fallen silent, and all the girls were looking at me expectantly. I floundered for what to say next, squinting against the autumn sunshine that was streaming in through the window.

'What a glorious view,' I began. 'The whole house is pretty amazing, don't you think?'

When my opening gambit seemed to bore them, I tried to make a joke of it. 'Don't tell me you all live in houses like this outside of term time?'

I hoped that might make them laugh, but almost all of them nodded as if that was a perfectly reasonable supposition.

'You don't, Japonica,' said one. I wondered whether she meant to belittle her friend. I hoped these girls weren't bullies.

Japonica was unperturbed. 'No, my house is much bigger.'

'Mine's the same size, but more modern,' said another.

'Yes, yours is a nice new house,' returned her companion. 'Everything brand new, not old, so it's cleaner and all its edges are straight. Not like our wonky old beams. Daddy says our minstrels' gallery is a death trap.'

'Is your house like this, Miss Lamb?' asked Japonica.

I was grateful to be spared from replying by a tap on my shoulder. It was Oriana, who had just dismissed her table.

'Good morning, Miss Lamb,' she said, a useful reminder to use only our surnames in front of the girls. 'I hope you slept well and are ready to face the new term.'

'Very well, thank you. And you?'

This mutual-concern habit was catching.

'Yes, thanks. And the girls have looked after you at breakfast?'

'Oh yes, they've been marvellous. Especially Imogen. I can see why they're all prefects.'

As a ripple of giggles went around the table, I realised they'd all finished eating and mine were the only pupils left in the Trough. I put my knife and fork together to indicate I was done too, although I wasn't.

'Thank you, girls, you may go.' It was rather pleasing to feel so powerful for a change. With a clatter of shifting chairs, they sped away, leaving me to chat to Oriana without an audience.

'I feel honoured to be put in charge of – or is it in the care of? – so many prefects.'

Oriana raised her immaculate eyebrows. 'Oh, Miss Lamb, did you not look around you at all? Did you spot a single girl who wasn't wearing a prefect's badge?'

I had to admit I hadn't.

When she sat down beside me to explain, I took the opportunity to sneak another forkful of egg.

'A father of a particularly undeserving daughter insisted she wouldn't return to the school for her final year unless she was made a prefect. The bursar was quick to agree, to make her father sign on the dotted line and stump up the annual fees. When Hairnet found out, she said she'd rather make every girl a prefect than honour that obnoxious man's child for the wrong reasons.'

I laughed. My respect for Miss Harnett was going up by the minute.

'I don't suppose the girls objected?'

'No, nor their parents. It'll look good on everybody's CV and adds perceived value to what they are getting in return for their school fees. Still, it's not as good as what happened in a similar incident three years ago.'

'What was that?'

'She made them all head girl.'

The school bell rang out, and Oriana leapt to her feet.

'Come on, or we'll be late for the staff briefing, and that's punishable by death.'

With a wistful look at the remains of my breakfast, I got up and followed her down to the staffroom. The eggs were good, but not worth that kind of sacrifice.

7

STAFF BRIEFING

Oriana had mastered the art of opening and closing the heavy school doors gently and quietly. Her slender arms hid remarkable strength. As the meeting was about to begin, she held the staffroom door open just wide enough for us to slip inside inconspicuously. I sidled to the back corner of the room, intending to survey the assembled group without them watching me.

But I couldn't take my eyes off Miss Harnett. She was mesmerising. I'd only met her once before, at my interview, and she'd left a powerful first impression.

The only other member of staff in school that day had been the bursar, a bland little man in his fifties. He had shown me through to Miss Harnett's ornate study, which he'd told me was the most lavish room in the house. Head's perks. I'd have picked the same if I'd been her. There we found her seated in a cerise velvet armchair, one hand cradling a fluffy black cat as big as a dog, the other hand repeatedly stroking its head. The fur on its skull gleamed like the shiny patch on a bronze statue that tourists touch for luck.

Beckoning me to sit on the hard brocade sofa opposite, she immediately began her gentle interrogations. My careful preparations wrong-footed me for Miss Harnett's line of questioning. She never once asked my views on the GCSE or A-level English syllabus, or the recent Nobel Prize winner for literature, or the current poet laureate. Instead she asked me about my parents and siblings, my attitude to animals and my favourite childhood memories. Her final question surprised me most: 'In a burning classroom, if you had time to rescue only one child, how would you choose which girl?'

I thought fast. The one nearest the door, I told her, as I'd have the greatest chance of success – and every one of them would be some parent's child, and most important in their eyes.

Then came a curious challenge: 'Demonstrate ten different ways to use a pashmina.'

She threw me a fuchsia pink one that lay in the cat's basket beside her armchair. Pretending I was a fashion vlogger, I improvised ten styles in quick succession, ending with a super-hero cape for her cat.

The cat purred its approval, so I left the pashmina on its back and returned to my perch on the sofa. I sat in silence awaiting further instructions while she admired her modishly attired cat. So long was the pause that I wondered whether the interview was over. Then she broke the silence so suddenly that I jumped.

'The job is yours, my dear. The bursar will be in touch with you about your contract, salary, conditions and so on, assuming you'd like to accept. I very much hope that you will.'

She fixed me with a winning smile.

'Yes, yes, I would, please. Thank you. Thank you so much. You've made me very happy.'

I hoped my gushing response didn't seem phoney. She just smiled, raised her hand, and wiggled her fingers in the direction of the door.

'Good girl. Now you may go.'

I stood up stiffly and stumbled over the crumpled fringe of the rug as I made my way to the door, anxious to escape. As I put my hand on the doorknob, Miss Harnett called after me.

'Miss Lamb.'

It was the first time I had been called that since my teaching practice. The memory made me smile. 'Do you know what clinched it for me?'

I assumed it was the cat's cape.

'Your warmth, Miss Lamb, your warmth. How much you care for others.'

Just as well I hadn't answered.

'It's not academic qualifications that make the world worth living in. It's human kindness. Did you know the modern structure of state education was originally devised to inculcate the Prussian Army into obedience and docility? Desks placed in military rows, strict uniforms to repress individuality, rote learning to stop you thinking for yourself – acts of cruelty and suppression, if you ask me.'

She leaned forward, tapping her chest. 'I didn't get where I am today by way of certificates. Do you know the most important thing I learned at prep school?'

I shook my head.

She beamed. 'How to steam open an envelope. And at senior school?'

I shrugged. I didn't dare guess.

'Not to sign anything I hadn't read.'

She sighed and turned away, gazing out of the window at the stunning floral displays immediately outside her study.

'And at university?' I ventured, feeling braver now I'd got the job.

She swivelled back sharply. 'My dear, university wasn't necessary in my day.' She'd waved a finger at me. 'Remember, kindness is all very well, but don't forget to put yourself first when you need to. You matter too.'

I'd given as big a smile as I could muster and fled before either of us could change our minds about the role.

* * *

Now I was in the staff room, buffered from Miss Harnett by my new colleagues, it was my turn to scrutinise her. I half-expected her to be wearing the pink pashmina in one of my ten fetching designs, but instead she sported a substantial black fur collar, despite the morning sunshine. Then the fur collar moved, and I recognised her feline sidekick. No one else seemed distracted by this odd fashion choice, all of them hanging on her every word as she began her start-of-term pep talk.

Halfway through, the cat jumped down from her neck, ambled across the floor, and weaved around my ankles. Mavis, clutching a stack of new exercise books to her chest, clad in a cardigan the colour of tumbleweed, shot me an envious look. I wouldn't have put her down as a cat person.

Having finished her speech, Miss Harnett flashed a smile around the room, then swept past me, scooped the cat up into her arms, and sailed out of the door.

'What does she call her cat?' I asked Mavis.

'McPhee,' said Mavis. 'As in *Nanny McPhee*. You know, the children's film in which the mysterious nanny turns up when you need her but don't want her?'

But there was no time to ask any more questions. My first lesson was about to begin.

8

THE STALKER

Not convinced that I could persuade the pupils as easily as I had Miss Harnett that I was a credible English teacher, I'd been swotting up. Revising the GCSE and A-level study guides for the appropriate exam board since before my interview, I was hoping to reverse-engineer lesson plans from them. Fortunately I was familiar with all of the set texts such as *Lord of the Flies* and *Macbeth*.

And even better luck awaited me in my stock cupboard, nestled in the corner of my classroom. Here I found not only the expected class sets of the books on the curriculum, but also pinned to the inside wall an outline lesson plan for the whole year. On a small table in the corner stood binders of more detailed lesson plans for each year group. My predecessor must have been efficient.

New exercise books, enough to distribute to every pupil, were in the English department's allocated colour of lavender. My favourite colour was everywhere: in my flat, in my classroom, in the uniform. It was a sign. Things were starting to go my way.

Handing out the exercise books to my first class, the youngest pupils, I realised they were even less certain than I was about how the lesson should proceed. These little girls wouldn't call me out if I got something wrong. They were happy to spend the first ten minutes writing their names in lavish curls and flourishes on the covers of their new exercise books while I drew a map of the classroom layout, noting who was sitting at which desk, so I could start to get to know them by name.

Then I led a discussion about what they'd read over the holidays and explained how to write book reviews. Their homework for the next lesson would be to write a review on the best book they'd read during the summer. Relieved that most of them seemed to have read at least one, I realised I'd have to get attuned to the jargon here. It was 'prep', short for preparation, rather than homework, because as boarders they didn't do it at home.

For the second lesson I had the next oldest class, who were keen to see that Daphne du Maurier's *Rebecca* was the first book on the curriculum – a promising start. Particularly pleased was a cheery auburn-haired girl named Rebecca, though she might not have been quite so cheery when she'd reached the end of the novel.

As per the lesson plan, after distributing the new exercise books and class set of novels, I set them the task of writing an essay in the style of a newspaper report on the most remark-able thing they had done during the summer holidays. They quickly set to work, emitting odd chuckles and gasps as they scribbled away, and I found myself looking forward to marking the results.

Could I really become a proper teacher at last? Perhaps I could. I had the right degree, the teaching qualification, the job. All I needed now was experience. Every teacher had been where I was now, and here I was too, starting to gain experience already. I was on my way. Perhaps taking this job had not been such a reckless idea after all – just so long as Steven didn't find me.

* * *

'Perhaps I should have specified that I wanted fact, not fiction.'

My free period first thing the next morning found me sitting at the staffroom table, red pen poised over an open lavender exercise book.

Joe, busy writing the new term dates for the next year in his planner, looked up and grinned. 'Why, what have they fobbed you off with? Missions to Mars? A fortnight on Atlantis?'

I laughed. 'Might just as well be. A month's scuba diving in the Cayman Islands. Cruising on a film star's yacht. House guest of a minor royal in the Scottish Highlands.'

Joe shrugged. 'It's how these kids roll. You'd better get used it.'

He reached over and pulled the next exercise book off the pile I had yet to read. As he flipped it open to the first page, I noticed it was still almost blank, with just a single sentence across the top in a curling hand reminiscent of Cyrillic.

Joe read aloud in a Russian accent, 'What I Did in My

Summer Holidays – This is classified information. You have insufficient privileges. Access denied.'

I was still smiling as I headed to my next class. This school was certainly different from any on my teaching practice placements, and so much more interesting. Plus everyone seemed to care about each other, staff and girls alike.

I found myself much more confident and relaxed for the next two lessons. I was enjoying getting to know the girls in each year group and their reactions to the texts we were due to discuss. The Y9s impressed me with their lively reading of the first few scenes of *A Midsummer Night's Dream*, our designated Shakespeare play for this term, injecting far more feeling and interest into the dialogue than I would expect from girls of their age. Then the Y11s awed me with their sensitive and insightful comments about Wilfred Owen's poem *Dulce et Decorum Est* from the First World War poetry on the curriculum for autumn. I would have to do something very bad indeed to fail my probation if all my classes were like this.

Morning break came around quickly, and feeling satisfied with my day so far, I settled down on the staffroom window seat to drink my coffee. I gazed down the winding drive, thinking how clever the landscape architect had been to design such tantalising views from the approach road. The meandering drive offered a different view of the mansion at every turn before the final dramatic reveal of its frontage from the forecourt.

It was equally tantalising for the residents to watch visitors arrive. Lord Bunting and his family must have been kept guessing as each new carriage approached, half-hidden by artfully planted foliage lining the drive. Now, glimpses of pillar-box red flashed in between the trees as a car wound its way towards the school.

'The postman comes a bit late here, doesn't he?' I said to Mavis, who was sitting at the other end of the window seat blowing on her steaming cup of coffee.

The staffroom coffee machine was like a caffeinated geyser, dispensing drinks so hot they were practically gaseous. As Mavis had showed me how to work it without scalding myself, she'd referred to it as Old Faithful. 'After the famously reliable hot-water spout in Yellowstone Park. So at least there's one thing in the school you can depend on.'

'The postman doesn't come at all,' she said now, clattering a silver spoon about in her cup, as if to beat her coffee into submission. 'First thing in the morning, Postman Joe fetches the school mailbag on his bike from the Slate Green sorting office and takes the outgoing post back after tea.'

'Postman Joe?'

I glanced across to the battered leather armchair in which he sat reading the jobs section of *The Times Educational Supplement*. He grinned.

'Forgotten me already, Gemma?' He winked and went back to his paper.

'Of course not.' In such a small community, I wanted to be friends with everyone. 'It's just that the vehicle coming through the trees over there looks like a post office delivery van. Well, it's that colour, anyway.'

Just like Steven's latest acquisition: a plush, silent electric sports car, the type more likely to be found outside a posh detached house than in the car park of a block of small modern flats like his. Steven probably hoped anyone who saw him driving it would assume he had the real estate to match. I'd thought it needlessly extravagant, but I'd long ago given up trying to influence his spending. After all, as he was quick to point out, it was his money, not mine.

I gazed at the red vehicle as it emerged on to the open part of the drive. Mavis was right. It was not a post office van, but a red car, a lot like Steven's. As it slowed down to cross the cattle grid, I noticed a light flash behind it, like a speed camera on the motorway. Max must have installed a security device to record the number plates of visiting cars. I pictured him tracking the stranger's progress on a surveillance screen somewhere in his underground lair.

Slowly I sipped my coffee, now at drinkable temperature, trying to convince myself that the sight of a car like Steven's should no longer cause me to panic. I was safe here. Wasn't I?

Then the car swung into the turning circle at the front of the house, slid into a visitors' parking space, and Steven stepped out, footsteps crunching ominously on the gravel.

Heart pounding, I leapt to my feet, forgetting about the coffee cup balanced on my lap, and spilled the contents all over my skirt. Chocolate-brown rivulets ran down my legs. I'd never realised a half-empty cup could hold so much coffee.

Joe jumped up and spread his newspaper on the floor in front of me and beckoned me to stand on it. I felt like a dog that had just been swimming in a muddy river. Coffee dripped off me like raindrops from an umbrella in a storm.

'You okay, Gemma? You're not scalded, I hope?'

'No, it's not that hot now. It's just... it's just that...'

How to explain my alarm without embarrassing myself?

'It's just there's someone out there who I don't want to see. He's not meant to know I'm here.'

Oriana sidled across from the staff noticeboard where she'd been reading the day's announcements. Oblivious to my comment, she looked languidly out of the window, peering round to see where the visitor had gone.

'Whose father is that handsome man? Must be a new girl's.'

The front doorbell echoed down the corridor from the entrance hall. Steven must be seeking admittance.

I groaned. 'He's not a girl's father. He's my ex-boyfriend, and I don't want to see him.'

Oriana raised her eyebrows. 'Why ever not? What's not to like? Smart car, expensive suit, good-looking.'

I didn't know what to say. Given half the chance, Steven would most likely charm her as he did everyone else. As he'd charmed me too, at first. No one would ever believe me if I so much as hinted at the truth about Steven.

Mavis drained her coffee cup.

'Not playing away, are you, Gemma?' she said. 'I wouldn't have put you down as the type to carry on with married men.' She flashed a contemptuous look at Oriana as the doorbell rang again.

'A male visitor? Does he have any daughters with him?' asked the bursar, coming to join us, morning coffee in hand. It was the bursar's duty to buzz visitors in via the intercom in his office, as the budget didn't run to a receptionist. No wonder Steven was getting no reply. 'We've still got a few spare places for this term. I'd better go and let him in.'

'No, Bursar, please don't!' I blurted out. 'He's not a prospective parent at all. He doesn't have any children. He's a merchant banker, with no legitimate business visiting St Bride's.'

Oriana fetched a hairbrush from her pigeonhole, although her hair looked tidy enough to me.

The bursar hesitated, and the doorbell sounded again. I realised I had no choice but to come clean, no matter the cost to my reputation.

'He's my ex-boyfriend, and I don't want to see him. Our relationship is completely over and I want no more to do with him. I've no idea what he's doing here, but I really don't want him to know I work here now.' Panicking at the prospect of Steven storming in and making a scene about the way I'd left him, I turned to Oriana, trying to conceal the extent of my fear by making a feeble joke. 'I would tell you "He's all yours if you want him!", Oriana, but believe me, you don't!'

She seemed unmoved. 'Shall I go and tell him he's made a mistake and that there's no Gemma Lamb here?'

Joe laughed. 'No, don't do that, Oriana. That'll only show him he's come to the right place. Just stonewall him and send him on his way.'

Oriana flashed me a beatific smile. 'I'm perfectly willing to create a diversion for you, Gemma.'

'I think Gemma's already done that herself,' said Joe, pointing at my caffeinated legs.

Fishing a packet of paper tissues from her jacket pocket, Nicolette knelt to pat my skirt dry. 'There, now you do not drip on the floor. Now, *vite*! *Vas y!*' She clapped her hands to hurry me along, as if I were one of her pupils. 'You just have time to change before the next lesson.'

Of course, that should be my priority. Never mind Steven. I'd be a laughing stock if I turned up to my classroom covered in brown stains.

'A merchant banker, you say?' Oriana's eyes shone. 'I'm free next period. I'm sure I can find plenty to talk about to distract him. You carry on, Gemma.'

Before I could object, she slipped her hairbrush into her pigeonhole, straightened her pencil skirt, and glided out of the staffroom door as if on castors, leaving me to scuttle away like a daddy-long-legs to the sanctuary of my flat, feeling guilty for not giving Oriana a stronger warning against Steven's controlling nature.

'So what was all that about this morning?' asked Joe gently, as we stood outside the Trough waiting for the girls to arrive for lunch.

I pursed my lips. I had hoped to be starting a new life here where people would know me only as me, rather than as Steven's appendage. In the absence of any better idea, I told him the truth.

'I left Steven because he was suffocating me.'

'Not literally, I hope?'

'No, but he might just as well have been. I realised a few months ago I was no longer my own person. Nor the person I wanted to be.'

Joe raised his eyebrows. 'I don't suppose he took kindly to your departure. What man of taste would?'

I looked away, wondering whether he thought I'd behaved

like a child. 'I don't know how he took it. You see, I haven't seen him since I moved out. I just left him a note to find when he came back from his business trip to Switzerland.'

'So you treated him like the milkman, telling him you no longer required his daily pint of gold top?' He laughed. 'Don't worry, Gemma, I'm only kidding, and I'm not judging you for a moment. I'm sure you had your reasons.'

I was glad he didn't press me to explain. 'I'm afraid so. I didn't leave a forwarding address either. You see, I didn't want him to come after me. I thought he'd never guess where I'd gone. He wouldn't even have heard of St Bride's. Nor had I, to be honest, until I saw the job ad online.' I sighed. 'I can't believe he worked it out. It's not as if I left a paper trail. All the correspondence about my application was done online.'

Joe narrowed his eyes, but there was a twinkle in them, as if he was teasing me. 'So how do you think he found you? Tracking device? Electronic tag?'

I frowned. 'Don't. I wouldn't put it past him to have microchipped me in my sleep.'

He grinned sympathetically.

'He's probably just guessed your email password. That wouldn't take a mastermind.'

'Oh, but that's the thing. He insisted we had a joint email account, as he had no secrets from me. In order to apply for jobs, I had to set up another one of my own that he didn't know about.'

Joe's smile faded. 'It's one thing to have no secrets from you, but quite another to deny you privacy. We're talking about basic human rights here.'

I hadn't thought of it like that before. I wouldn't make that mistake again.

'Perhaps he cracked your secret email too if he was keeping you on such a short lead.'

My face must have fallen, because he put his hand to his mouth.

'Sorry, that's not an appropriate analogy. I'm not for a moment comparing you to a dog.'

'That's nothing, Steven's called me much worse. But I still don't see how he could have found me. I only ever accessed my secret email at the local library.'

'How about your search history at home? I'm guessing you shared a computer. Even if you didn't use it for your secret email, did you ever use it to view the school's website?'

I closed my eyes as if that might shut out the truth. 'How could I be so stupid! I should have used one of those secret search settings. What do they call it?'

'Incognito. But don't worry, just tell Max to keep him off the school premises and you'll be fine.'

'Really? You think Max can keep him out?'

Joe didn't know how persistent Steven could be.

High heels tapping across the parquet floor heralded the arrival of Oriana, looking pleased with herself.

'I headed him off at the pass for you, Gemma.' She was twisting Steven's business card between her long varnished nails.

'Whatever did you do with him, Oriana?' I pictured an impossible scene: his scarlet car on its roof in a ditch, wheels spinning, after a hefty blow from her strong arms.

'He told me he was looking for a bookish girl called

Gemma Lamb at a place called St Bride's, but was confused because he'd advised her not to get a job at a school. I told him he'd got the wrong St Bride's and sent him off down the road.'

'There's another St Bride's School near here? That must cause confusion.'

Joe laughed and put his hand on my shoulder. 'Welcome to our parallel universe, Gemma.'

'Don't be so stupid, Joe.' Oriana slapped his chest with the back of her hand. 'No, there's a church called St Bride's a couple of miles away. That's why the school's called St Bride's. We're in its parish.'

Joe grinned. 'The founding governors of the school, in their wisdom, thought the name suggested an educational institution full of unsullied, eligible maidens. A veritable Virgin Megastore of its day.'

Mavis caught the end of the conversation as she strode across the hall to join us. 'Yes, the dirty old gits.'

I still needed assurance from Oriana. 'How did you convince Steven he might find me in a church?'

Oriana focused on the cuticles of her left hand, pushing them back with the long nail of her right forefinger. 'There's a bookshop almost opposite the church. I can't remember its name, I never go there, but I thought he might believe you would get a job in a bookshop. Joe, you told me there's a new girl started work there recently? I might easily have thought she was the person he was looking for.'

Joe folded his arms. 'If you're talking about Sophie Sayers, she's been there at least a year.'

'Even so, I wasn't telling lies. Besides, it got him off your scent, Gemma, so job done.'

'Oh, charming!' said Joe. 'You're making her sound like a skunk. That's even worse than me calling her a dog just now.'

Mavis pushed past all three of us to open the Trough door, pausing only to say over her shoulder, 'And you, my dear Oriana, are nothing but a fox.'

9

RESPITE

The girls' conversation at lunch provided a welcome diversion, taking my mind off Steven. Every time I thought of him, my hands began to tremble.

'What's your name again, miss?' asked a small, dark-haired child with big round eyes.

Another pupil answered before I could. 'It's Miss Lamb, silly. Don't you remember? Hairnet said the way to remember it is to think of a sweet, gentle creature who wouldn't harm a soul.'

As ever, I was intrigued by Miss Harnett's methods.

'How does she tell you to remember the rest of the staff's names?'

The first girl laid her knife and fork across her empty plate.

'Miss Bliss always looks like she's just stepped out of a beauty parlour, so we're to think of the bliss of sinking into a pamper session.'

'Or a hot bath,' piped up another. 'She always looks very clean and shiny.'

'And she always smells nice,' said another.

'Miss Brook is easy because a brook is a geographical feature you might find on a map, and she teaches us geography.'

'And Mr Spryke?'

'You mean Miss Spryke, silly,' said Tilly, one of the smallest girls at the table. A couple of older girls listening in from the next table exchanged knowing looks. I wondered how aware they were of the truth about Joe.

Three of the little ones chorused together: 'Miss Spryke rides her bike.' The older girls sniggered, making me almost certain they knew about Joe's disguise

I wondered whether Joe's bike was a man's model with a crossbar, or a genteel ladies' model with a wicker basket on the front.

'Does Miss Harnett have the same system for the teachers' first names, too?' I was curious as to what they'd make of Oriana. I'd never met anyone called Oriana before.

The first girl leaned into me, wide-eyed.

'Oh, Miss Lamb, none of us are allowed to know teachers' first names. It's against the school rules.'

'Mind you, we're pretty sure we know what they all are,' said the second. 'We're good at guessing and solving clues.'

'So whose names have you guessed?'

'Miss Bliss' name. It begins with an O, and we think it's Obergine, because we heard Miss Brook saying to Miss Spryke at lunch one day that she can't stand Obergine. And it's true, Miss Bliss and Miss Brook detest each other, everyone knows that.'

'And what about Miss Brook's first name?'

'We think it's probably the name of a famous mountain. She told us once that she became a geography teacher because when she was a little girl, her parents liked taking her to mountainous places on holiday.'

'I bet she was conceived on one,' said one of the older girls behind us, before falling into fits of giggles with her companions.

'There are loads of mountains beginning with M, because we looked them up in the atlas. Like Mount Mackenzie. We've got a jigsaw puzzle of it in our common room. It's in Canada. The mountain, not our common room.'

'There's a Magic Mountain in Washington. Wouldn't that be a cool name, Magic Brook? It sounds like somewhere unicorns go to drink.'

'My money's on Matterhorn,' Joe said, leaning over from his table, from which he'd just dismissed his girls. They were faster eaters and less chatty than mine. 'I think it would rather suit Miss Brook, don't you, girls, with her snowy peak?'

'Oh, but Miss Spryke, she wouldn't have had white hair when she was born, would she?'

Imogen pulled a notepad out of her blazer pocket and checked a scribbled list. 'Matterhorn's got the best odds at the moment.'

I hoped they might go on to reveal the mysterious Caroline's surname, but then a bell sounded in the hall, prompting the girls to shovel down the rest of their apple crumble so that I could dismiss them.

Once they'd gone, I turned to Joe.

'So why aren't the girls allowed to know our first names, Miss Spryke?'

Joe grinned.

'It distracts them from trying to find out more valuable personal information, such as our PIN numbers or our passwords for the school computer network. Another of Hairnet's creative educational strategies.'

Joe scraped back his chair and stood up. I did the same, realising we were the last to leave the Trough.

'Coming to join me for coffee in the staffroom before next lesson, or has this morning's incident put you right off Old Faithful's eruptions?'

I hesitated. 'Actually I think I need a bit of solitude to get my head together before class. I still feel a bit shaken by Steven's surprise appearance this morning.'

That was an understatement.

'Ah, solitude. Not easy to come by while school's in session, though it's a great space for chilling outside of term time. That's another reason I occasionally jump on my bike and pedal off into the sunset – for the opportunity to think. Wherever you are in school, you can never entirely relax because a girl might come knocking on your door in a state of need.'

I thought for a moment.

'There must be some parts of the school where you're less likely to be interrupted by the girls?'

He considered. 'You could try the library. The girls don't use it much at lunchtime. Or the mausoleum – you know, where Lord Bunting rests? It's out of bounds to the girls except on Founder's Day. Although it's a bit chilly, it's less musty and dusty than the library. Well, there is dust, but it's sealed up tight in the old boy's tomb.'

I wrinkled my nose. 'I'll try the mausoleum, then. As long as you can swear it's not haunted.'

Joe laughed. 'You're as credulous as the kids. You'd better hurry, though, as it's only fifteen minutes before afternoon lessons begin.'

10

DEAD HONEST

I strode across the springy lawn to the mausoleum, a minute's brisk walk from the Trough. After heaving open the old oak door and pushing aside the thick velvet curtain, I swung the door closed behind me. The clang as the lock hit the door jamb ricocheted off the chilly marble-lined walls.

Alone for this visit, I studied the small entrance space. Low light filtered in through tiny arrow slits and high stained-glass windows near the roof. I looked down at myself, pale grey in the shadow. It was like seeing my own ghost.

The cool, shadowy atmosphere was restful for the dead at least. The school bell, as dependable as Big Ben, would never penetrate these thick walls, nor would anyone outside hear what went on within. But for some reason, I felt on edge.

I swallowed hard and walked around the corner, making my way towards Lord Bunting's tomb with a boldness I did not feel. It might be interesting, I told myself, to become better acquainted with him. The calm profile of the old man's alabaster effigy suggested his satisfaction with his life's achievements. I ran my fingers along his intricately carved robes, the work of a master sculptor.

How sad for Lord Bunting that his beloved wife had opted not to join him in this place of rest. What a different society she lived in, in which a man's proposal of marriage included what he offered beyond the grave. Happier for Lady Bunting, however, to find a new love, even if it meant the second plinth would remain forever vacant.

Or not. As I turned away from Lord Bunting's tomb, intending to cast a sympathetic glance at the empty plinth, I drew in a sharp breath of surprise. For there, in a pose mirroring Lord Bunting's, lay the unmistakable figure of Miss Harnett, McPhee curled up at her feet like the dog on the tomb of a crusader.

In contrast to Lord Bunting's cream alabaster robes, Miss Harnett was wearing a red tartan skirt-suit and a multi-coloured floral silk scarf. She hadn't moved since my arrival, so I assumed she was either asleep or deep in a meditative trance. Suddenly her eyes flicked open and she sat up.

'Gemma, my dear, you startled me. I didn't hear you come in. Have you come to let off steam where no one can hear you? Good for you.'

'I— I'm sorry, Miss Harnett, I didn't mean to disturb you.'

She swung her legs round to step carefully down on to the tiled floor.

'Not at all, my dear. I just slip down here now and again to draw strength and inspiration from dear Lord Bunting, especially at the start of a new school term. Lying here beside him,

I can feel his energies, like ley lines, shooting through my body.'

For a moment, I wondered whether they had been secret lovers, until I realised he was at least a hundred years her senior.

'Was he an educational expert? I thought his house and grounds became an educational establishment only after his death.'

'In a way, you are right, Gemma. He was simply a gentleman, going about his business as an engineer, inventor, and landowner, living on his patent fees, rents, and dividends. But that didn't preclude him from also being a man of vision, commissioning this beautiful house and its gardens even though he knew he'd never live long enough to see it reach maturity. When he died, all that weathered old Cotswold stone was still as fresh as when it was cut from the Slate Green quarry, and the trees that tower above us now were mere saplings.'

She looked up to the stained-glass windows.

'But his influence spread far beyond St Bride's. His inventions shaped the nation's infrastructure for future generations. They still do today.'

She stepped across the aisle to lay her hands gratefully on his own.

'There are many parallels between him and me. As he did with his inventions, I cast my girls out into the world. And just as he planted his gardens with only an inkling of how they'd look at maturity, I can only guess at the ultimate destiny of my girls. I just hope and pray that they will flourish and thrive.'

'But surely you know how some of them fare? Don't they keep in touch? You could always befriend them on social media to keep track of them.'

'Some write to me after they've left, but many don't. As for social media, my dear, I steer clear of it. I'm sure it does far more harm than good. It's no substitute for a proper letter.'

I suppose a headmistress's work is just the start of the story. It must be like mixing up so many fairy cakes, putting them in the oven, but never being around when the timer rings to see which have sunk or risen, or what decorations will adorn them once they've had a chance to cool on the wire rack.

'The girls' exam results must give you a certain indication of their future destiny?'

Miss Harnett sighed as she lifted her still-sleeping cat from the second plinth and cradled him in her arms.

'My dear, how often must I tell you? Exams count for nothing here. Of course, the girls all take them, and we prepare and encourage them as best we can. But all public exams do is tell you who is good at passing tests, and which teachers are best at brainwashing or bullying their pupils into submission. I've seen straight-A pupils end up in dire straits, and dunces go on to shine. Exam results are no indication of our true chances in life. It's what's in your heart, not your head, that makes the difference. Which is probably just as well for us all.'

'So if not exam results, what do you see as the girls' most important achievements?'

I was genuinely interested, thinking it politic to align my teaching, such as it was, with her philosophy, at least while I was in her employ.

She strolled around the corner, towards the door, and I followed.

'We teach them to be kind, to be caring, to be interested in the world about them. To value beauty, art, and culture. To be opportunists, to be enterprising, creative, and inventive, to make the most of their individual passions. More than one girl here is already running a lucrative online business, you know.'

'Lord Bunting certainly provided the perfect setting in which to nurture talents, although perhaps it's not where a teenager would choose to live.'

'No bright lights, you mean? No shops, no bars, no night-clubs? Don't you believe it. They'll have plenty of time for such things later. Many have more than enough of them in the school holidays. Some find it a blessed relief to return here each term, ditching their make-up and their hair straighteners and on-trend clothes for the sake of returning to a childlike state. They're in no hurry to grow up. So, my dear, I'll leave you in peace here to ponder on our conversation. You have five minutes before afternoon lessons begin.'

When she'd closed the door behind her, I leaned back against the velvet curtain, pressing my fingers into the comforting pile, and breathed a sigh of relief at being on my own again. Apart from Lord Bunting, of course. I wondered how many curious conversations he had overheard from his slab, how many confidences lonely or anxious staff had whispered into his stone ear. I could do worse than share mine with him.

Returning to his side, I stroked the bridge of his Roman nose, then ran a finger over his high cheekbones. The sculptor had etched smile lines about his wide, thin-lipped mouth and at the corners of his heavily-hooded closed eyes. I decided I would have liked him in real life. Patting his clasped hands companionably, I was just considering testing the empty plinth for myself when the banging of a door jolted me out of my reverie. It was not loud enough to be the main door, but I hadn't noticed another one.

Gripping Lord Bunting's hands for moral support, I jerked round just in time to see Max, wearing a head torch, emerging from what looked like a wardrobe set into the wall behind the plinths.

'Oh my goodness, Max, you frightened me!'

When I shielded my eyes from the dazzling torch beam, he reached up to turn it off.

'Stealth is my middle name. But I didn't mean to startle you. I just wanted to check you were okay now that the boss has gone.'

I left Lord Bunting's side to investigate Max's wardrobe, or cupboard, or whatever it was. Beyond the doors were steps leading down through pitch darkness.

'Is this another exit from your tunnel network?'

'Lord Bunting's network of tunnels.' He turned to give a military salute to the effigy. 'Although there's only one other exit to this particular tunnel.'

'So you can pop up anywhere, any time?'

He stood to attention and clicked his heels.

'Never more than a scream away, that's me.'

I took great comfort from that notion. I'd be safer from Steven at St Bride's than at anywhere else I might live and work. Then Max glanced at his vast and complicated watch.

'By the way, you'd better get to your classroom. The bell for the next lesson will just be ringing.'

And with that he flicked his head torch back on, stepped behind the doors, and closed the latch from within. When I opened the door a moment later, he'd vanished like a magician's assistant in a trick wardrobe.

11

MCPHEE

The next morning I awoke to find a heavy weight pinning down the duvet alongside my right thigh. Wondering what on earth it might be, I kept my eyes tightly shut, racking my brains for a harmless explanation.

It was far too heavy to be the novel I'd been reading as I fell asleep the night before. Surely it couldn't be the school governor that Oriana had warned me against, but who else could it be? I'd gone to bed alone. Did Max have a secret entrance to my flat? It could hardly link to one of Lord Bunting's underground tunnels, as my flat was upstairs. Mavis had called Joe an old goat. At the time I hadn't thought of it in a threatening way, but was that what she had meant? Had Joe drugged my coffee in the staffroom after dinner, and was now sleeping off his conquest beside me? I shuddered.

As I tried to edge away, the lump stirred and settled down again. My eyes still closed, I reached one hand out from beneath the duvet in search of a clue. My fingertips encountered something warm, furry, and steadily vibrating.

I opened my eyes to find a purring McPhee curled up like a hibernating squirrel, the tip of his tail touching his ears with commendable neatness. How long had he been there, and, more importantly, how had he got in? I had no recollection of admitting him. I'd kept my windows closed, and the front door to my flat was still firmly shut and bolted. Were there other means of gaining access to my room? Secret passageways behind the wooden panelling of the upstairs corridors, beyond the reach of the underground tunnels? Was Max not the only one who knew his way around them?

I sighed. No, I was letting my imagination run away with me. Cats moved on silent paws. McPhee must have followed me into my flat the night before, when I was too distracted and emotionally drained to notice before falling into bed.

McPhee opened his eyes, and as I stroked his soft black back, the volume of his purr increased. Miss Harnett might have been missing him, even if McPhee wasn't missing Miss Harnett. I realised I should return him straight away.

Suddenly McPhee sat up and pricked up his ears. A split second later, the school bell rang, and I glanced at my watch. It was 7.45 a.m., which meant this was the fifteen-minute warning bell for breakfast. Realising I had slept through the 7 a.m. wake-up bell, I threw back the covers and scrambled into action, leaving McPhee rolling over on to his back and stretching out his paws.

Within ten minutes I was washed and dressed, which gave me five minutes to return McPhee to Miss Harnett's study before breakfast. With the cat bundled in my arms, I tiptoed down the carpeted hall and stooped to set him gently down by the closed door. McPhee promptly gave the game away by miaowing loudly and plaintively.

'Just coming, darling,' said Miss Harnett from within. Soft footsteps pattered across the deep pile carpet towards us. Wary of making too much noise or looking foolish by sprinting away, I was still standing there when Miss Harnett opened the door.

Her eyes honed in on the cat and she beamed at the sight of him. McPhee trotted in contentedly as if this was all part of his plan, brushing affectionately against Miss Harnett's ankles on the way to his food dish beside her desk. A moment later, he was crunching cat biscuits. It was McPhee's breakfast time too.

Only then did Miss Harnett acknowledge my presence. I assumed she'd want an explanation.

'I'm sorry, I hope you didn't think McPhee was lost. I just found him on my bed when I woke up this morning. I've no idea how he got in. He wasn't there when I went to bed last night.'

Miss Harnett smiled like a proud parent who's just been told their child has won a house point for helpfulness.

'Ah, that's McPhee for you. Appears out of nowhere when you need her. But when you want her and don't need her, she's nowhere to be found.'

She? Her? I didn't know much about animals, but when McPhee had displayed his fluffy tummy, paws in the air on my duvet, I had been sure he was a boy.

The breakfast bell rang before I could reply.

'Go on, then, off you trot. The girls will be waiting for you, and I have pressing work to do myself.'

She glanced down at her usually tidy desk, now covered in printouts of financial spreadsheets on which most of the figures appeared in red. I must have gawped in alarm at this evidence of the school's shaky financial situation, and she had to cough to gain my attention before waggling her fingers at the corridor to send me on my way. As I marched down towards the Trough, I began to fear that the school might not after all be the safe haven I had taken it for if its finances were as dire as those figures made it look.

* * *

'Good night's sleep, Miss Lamb?' called Joe cheerily from his table as I took my usual place at the head of mine.

I forced a smile.

'Fine, thanks, Miss Spryke. That is, until I woke up to find a large black cat curled up on my bed.'

Joe grinned. 'Lucky cat.'

'I've no idea how he got into my room.'

'Just wandered in behind you, I expect. She's done that to me before. Silent as a shadow, is McPhee.'

'She? But McPhee is a boy. I've seen his – I've seen the evidence.'

Joe winked. 'Remember the school marketing strategy. While school's in session, McPhee is female, like the rest of us.'

Before I had a chance to press Joe further, the girls returned from the serving hatch, bringing their breakfasts, and I was left to wonder at the wisdom of it all in my head.

With breakfast over, to my relief, the morning's lessons went smoothly, with the girls having mostly done their prep.

They were more than willing to talk about their new set texts. Their compliance couldn't all have been down to the effectiveness of Miss Harnett's policies. Perhaps I'd make a better teacher than I'd allowed myself to believe.

Break in the staffroom was considerably more relaxing than the day before, and I took the opportunity to press Oriana for more information about her encounter with Steven. She was dismissive.

'Oh, stop worrying, Gemma. I don't think he was even interested in you any more, not once I'd finished with him. It wouldn't surprise me if he didn't even go to that bookshop to try to find you. Just relax and leave him to me.'

Leave him to her? So had she set her sights on him now? Was that her ultimate diversionary tactic? As she headed off to teach her next lesson, I chastised myself for not warning her off Steven for her own sake, never mind mine. I'd have to pick the right moment later on.

Although Oriana was teaching, I had the next lesson free, and I was determined to spend it exploring the school library to search for further teaching resources. With the curriculum appearing to consist of classics, I hoped the library might offer more modern reading material for the girls to enjoy during their leisure time. I might even find some good books to read myself, having left most of mine at Steven's flat, taking only what I could fit in my car. I wondered whether Steven had even noticed what had gone.

12

LIBRARY STEPS

The library was a large, high-ceilinged room with vast bay windows offering breathtaking views of the gardens on two sides. Sumptuously padded window seats were scattered with velvet cushions the same faded shade of maroon as the leather bindings of the antique books on the highest shelves. The lower shelves, within a girl's arm's reach, carried modern editions more likely to appeal to twenty-first-century teenage readers. Finding the fiction section, I discovered quite a few novels that might provide useful reading around the curriculum. I wondered how often the girls borrowed books from the library.

The girls were certainly conspicuous by their absence. When I saw a handwritten list of library rules pinned to a noticeboard beside the fireplace, I understood why. 'No talking, no shouting, no whispering, no giggling, no phones, no music, no tapping of feet or pencils, no dark glasses, no eating or drinking, no sweets, no littering.' It might just as well have said 'No girls.'

But as I gazed up to the ornate plasterwork on the ceiling with its swags of colourless fruit and flowers, I realised I was not alone. At the top of a set of library steps, tall enough to reach the highest shelf, stood Mavis Brook, examining one of a dozen identical leather-covered volumes.

'Are those class sets?' I called up to her.

Mavis steadied herself on the pole at the top of the steps. 'No, they're all completely different on the inside. Just the covers are the same.'

She tucked the book under her arm and began to descend.

'They're strictly out of bounds to the girls, by the way. We can't risk them going up and down this ladder. I dice with death every time I come up here myself, but at least if I fall to the floor, my parents won't sue the school.'

She looked relieved to reach the ground.

'Not that the girls are bothered. Given their choice, they'd bypass books altogether and gather all their knowledge from the internet.' She spat that last word out as if it were an obscenity. 'Blasted internet! More trouble than it's worth. Most of what's on the internet is nonsense anyway, or plain wrong. What did the internet ever do for us?'

I bit back a smile. 'What about Google Maps? I'd have thought that was a gift to a geographer. And GPS. And Google Earth. Live images to take your pupils to places you could never visit on a field trip.'

Mavis sighed in exasperation, as if dealing with an argumentative pupil. 'Oh, for goodness' sake, Gemma, you can't beat a good book, especially modern books with all their colour pictures and glossy covers – unlike these dusty old doorstops. Cheery fonts and pristine pages! I wish I'd had some like that when I was at school.'

I looked up at the antique tomes on the higher shelves. There must have been hundreds of them. 'So why does the school keep all those old titles?'

She waved the one she had brought down with her. I was curious to see what she'd chosen, presumably a classic geographical publication or an early atlas, but its spine was facing away from me.

'They came with the house, as part of Lord Bunting's legacy to the new school foundation. Of course, he was clueless as to what kinds of books a school would need, and quite possibly never read these books himself. They were just standard issue for a gentleman's country library. Even so, we should be grateful to him. They fill the space and they impress visiting parents, making our library resources look better endowed than they are and making us look more cultured.'

She walked to the supervisor's desk at the far end of the room, where a notebook lay open under the green glass table lamp. She set the book on the desk beside it, sat down, and picked up her fountain pen. I went across to sit at the spare chair opposite her, hoping she would tell me more about the school's benefactor. The more I found out about him, the fonder I became.

'So why do Lord Bunting's books all look the same?' I glanced up at the rows and rows of maroon spines.

'It was the fashion in those days. Printers produced identical insides, but the covers were made to the buyer's specification, to match their interior decor. Not that there was much choice: just the shade of leather and the exact wording on the cover.'

'I can see it makes them look nice and tidy, but how did they ever find what they were looking for? It would be like looking for a particular piece of hay in a haystack.'

Mavis opened the book at the title page and wrote down its title, author, and other details. I wondered whether she was cataloguing the collection. I'd read novels in which impoverished young men and women were retained to catalogue libraries in stately homes, like Eve Halliday at P. G. Wodehouse's Blandings, and now I understood why there'd be the need.

'They must gather a lot of dust up there,' I mused, observing the little grey halo that had settled around the book on the desk.

'Yes, they do. That's what I was doing up there. Dusting.' I noticed she didn't carry a duster. She patted the book, releasing a further cloud of fallout, and gave a wan smile. 'It's a glamorous life being a school librarian. That's my Extra, you know.'

Most of the teachers had at least one extra duty in their job description, besides their teaching workload. Each Extra provided a small increment to their salary and an additional achievement for their curriculum vitae, should they apply for another job. My Extra was fire drill officer, for which I'd received no training, apart from the bursar thrusting into my hands a hardback notebook listing the names of staff and pupils in alphabetical order. My duty was to record the names of the missing, rather than to take any preventative action, unless the fire was small enough for me to put out by smothering it with the notebook.

I looked again at the rows of leather-bound books above our heads, wondering how many had lain undisturbed, bar Mavis's dusting, since Lord Bunting's death. They must be falling to bits inside and would go up in flames like tinder. Here and there gaps in an otherwise perfectly matched set reminded me of toothpaste adverts, the ones that try to frighten you with images of beautiful models with missing teeth. I hoped the gaps in the bookshelves might act as firebreaks.

Then I remembered why I'd come here in the first place and stood up, brandishing my pile of essays and my mark book. 'Would it be okay if I did a bit of marking in here sometimes, for a change of scene from my classroom and the staffroom? It's such a lovely room.'

Mavis looked as if she did mind, but she shook her head anyway. 'Of course. This room is shamefully underused and undervalued.' I suspected she may have hoped to keep it that way, to remain mistress of all she surveyed. Understanding how precious privacy was in this place, I didn't want to impose.

'But I won't stop now.' I looked at my watch, to give the impression that I was pushed for time. 'Thanks anyway.'

As I stood up, Mavis pulled a large padded envelope from a desk drawer, big enough to take the book she had in front of her, the address already written on the front. Seeing me look, she flipped the envelope over to hide the address, but too late – I'd already read the first line: the name of an antiquarian bookshop in Oxford.

13

TEA FOR TWO

On the next day came a welcome afternoon off, at least for the staff who were not housemistresses. Thursday afternoons were set aside for teaching Life Skills. Given that this was a private school 'for young ladies', as Lord Bunting had specified, one might have expected these lessons to be in the style of a finishing school, such as teaching deportment, elocution, and getting out of a sports car without showing your knickers. In fact they were more socially-minded, as Miss Harnett had explained at my interview. The girls were despatched after lunch to local organisations happy to receive their help: nursing homes, charity shops, primary schools, preschools, and public parks. Each girl took a turn in the different sectors.

'It encourages the girls to consider the needs of others less fortunate than themselves,' she'd explained. 'Consequently in later life, a St Bridean would be the one to pick you up in the street if you fell over.'

Watching the girls from the staffroom window as they lined up on the forecourt, ready to board minibuses to their

Life Skills venues, I couldn't help but admire Miss Harnett's benevolent principles.

'I do think these Thursday afternoon outings are a wonderful idea,' I said to no one in particular.

'Yes,' said the bursar, topping up his cup at Old Faithful. 'Helping the local community validates our charity status, which reduces the burden of taxation.'

And there was me thinking the school's motive was purely philanthropic. I supposed every little saving helped if the school's finances were in as dire straits as those spreadsheets on Miss Harnett's desk had suggested.

The door flew open and Joe bounded in, making a beeline for me. He took the empty coffee cup from my hands and set it back on the trolley.

'Come on, you. It's a glorious day out there. I thought we could go for a bike ride.'

Mavis, rifling through her pigeonhole, turned to fix him with a glare.

'Stop bossing her about, Joe. Gemma might have other plans.'

Joe turned to me for adjudication. 'Did you have other plans for this afternoon, Gemma?'

'Er, no, actually,' I faltered, wondering whether I should invent some.

'Well, there's no time to hang about,' he said. 'We've only got till supper, when the hordes return.'

I stalled, nervous of leaving the premises for the first time since I'd arrived. What if Steven was still lurking about somewhere?

'But I don't have a bicycle.'

'No, but Oriana does, don't you, Oriana?'

Oriana scooped up the registers, ready to take the roll call prior to the girls' departure.

'You're welcome to my bike if you want it, Gemma. It's been rusting away in the bike shed for years. My cycling days are done. My current vehicle of choice is a sports car or private jet.'

Mavis tutted, stuffed her post back in her pigeonhole, and left the room.

'Well?' Joe was waiting for my decision.

'Just give me a few minutes to change. I can't cycle in a skirt.'

'Doesn't stop me.' He glanced down at his tennis dress. 'But if you must, I'll meet you in ten minutes round the back of the bike shed.'

'His natural habitat, naughty boy,' murmured Oriana, as she headed out of the door.

As I approached the bike shed in jeans and trainers, I wondered whether I'd made the right decision. I hadn't been on a bicycle for years. As a former professional cyclist, Joe might soon get fed up with me. I hoped he was planning a gentle ride around the school grounds, rather than a major expedition. The front drive alone was about a mile long, so we could easily do two miles without leaving the premises.

But Joe, dressed in black cycling shorts and a black water-proof jacket, had other ideas. 'We're going to Wendlebury

Barrow,' he announced, laying down the rag with which he'd been cleaning Oriana's bike. 'As head of English, you need to befriend the local bookshop.'

'Hang on.' A sudden thought popped into my head. 'Isn't that where Oriana diverted Steven to? I don't want to risk bumping into him.' I shuddered.

'Don't be daft. That was two days ago. They'll have told him straight away that they'd never heard of you because that would be the truth and he'll have gone on his way. I hardly think he's likely to loiter about the place on the off-chance that they're lying and you'll turn up. And in the very unlikely event that he is, you still wouldn't have to worry, because you've got me with you. I'd look after you.'

I was taken aback by his kindness.

'Thanks, Joe, I really appreciate that.'

He smiled.

'More to the point, the bookshop tearoom does a luscious afternoon tea.' This was the kind of coercion I could handle. 'And as you'll have cycled there, you can eat all the cake you like with a clear conscience.'

Lean, muscular Joe was the last person to have to worry about calories in cake. But I was persuaded.

'Sounds perfect. Thank you.'

As he wheeled Oriana's bike over to me, I asked, 'Which bike is yours?'

He pointed at a rack of six gleaming bicycles.

'All of them.'

'Wow.'

He extracted a broad-tyred traditional model from among

the high tech, highly sprung mountain bikes and lean, minimalist racers. I was glad we'd be on an equal footing, rather than him sleek and speedy, head bowed for aerodynamics, with me looking prim and proper behind.

Joe obviously enjoyed maintaining his bicycle collection, because, when I peered inside the shed, I could see neatly arranged boxes of tools, accessories and spares on the shelves. I guessed this was where one might find him in free periods and wondered what else went on here. Smoking, obviously. Cigarette ends littered the ground around the door.

Gingerly I stepped astride Oriana's bike.

'I may need a moment to get used to it.'

I lowered myself on to the saddle, grateful for its generous padding. I was also glad that this was an elegant upright model of vintage design with a pretty wicker basket on the front, rather than a racing machine. He could not expect me to reach high speeds on this bike.

'Don't worry,' said Joe, sensitive to my unease. 'It's an easy ride. The roads will be practically empty at this time of day. And there's no rush.'

We set off, Joe pedalling in swift circles around me as I teetered along the broad path that would take us on to the main drive.

'We can chat as we go,' he said, breathing as easily as if he were sitting in his staffroom armchair with his feet up. I hoped the chat would take my mind off the physical effort required to propel myself along.

We slowed down as we approached the twin gatehouses at the junction with the main road. This pair of mirror-image cottages stood sentry either side of tall wrought-iron gates. I stuck out my left hand to give a clear signal, surprised by the latent memory of cycling proficiency training at the age of thirteen. Joe glanced back over his shoulder and laughed at me.

'There's no one around to see you indicate except me. And I know where you're going.'

I stopped, put my feet on the ground, and he glided past, braking just in front of me.

'What about Max? Won't he have us on his radar?'

As if in reply, a net curtain twitched in the front window of one of the lodges. I nodded in that direction.

'Is that where Max lives?'

Joe shook his head. 'He and Rosemary live in the other one.'

'So who lives in that lodge?'

'The bursar.'

Although not huge, the lodges were quaint and pretty, with lattice-paned gothic windows arching beneath the dense thatch. I imagined that if sold off as private housing, they could earn the school quite a windfall, perhaps enough to lift it out of its current financial difficulties. I wondered whether I dared suggest it to Miss Harnett without incurring her wrath. I doubted the bursar would be keen on the idea as it would leave him homeless. Still, if it meant saving the school, perhaps needs must.

We pulled out on to the empty road. As we got up speed, a refreshing breeze cooled my glowing face, and I began to enjoy the journey. Soon my grip on the handlebars relaxed, and I felt sufficiently stable to turn my head to admire the scattered cottages and farmhouses along the way. The only traffic we saw was a tractor on the other side of the road and a couple of women on horseback riding side by side. Both of them raised a friendly hand in greeting, which I returned with only a slight wobble of my bike.

After a few miles, we reached a junction and paused to allow a few cars to come and go before crossing over the road. Within a few hundred metres, we passed a sign saying: 'Welcome to Wendlebury Barrow.' Then came the beginnings of an ancient ribbon development of old stone cottages, with a couple of side roads leading to newer housing developments behind.

After we'd passed a shop and a pub, Joe cycled ahead of me to lead the way. When he gave an elaborate wave of his right hand, the 'I'm slowing down' sign, I wondered whether he was teasing me. Then he stuck out his left hand and pulled over outside the bookshop, above which a hanging sign announced:

TEA
CAKE
BOOKS

He leaned his bike against the side of the building, slipping it deftly between the wall and a Land Rover parked alongside the shop. Then he turned to take mine and propped it up against his. The two machines nestled intimately together, handlebars against saddles, pedal against pedal. I dropped my helmet into Oriana's wicker basket and ran my fingers through my hair to plump it up, my scalp warm and damp from the exertion.

'Come on, then.' He led the way, holding the door open for me to enter the shop.

I hesitated. 'Aren't you going to lock the bikes up?'

Joe shook his head. 'No need round here; they'll be safe enough while we have our tea.'

Just inside the door, a man in his early thirties with dark curly hair and clear green eyes looked up from behind the counter, where he'd been tapping away at a computer keyboard. He smiled when he saw Joe, then at me.

'Hi, Joe, who's your friend?'

'She can talk, you know,' said Joe. That was refreshing. Steven would have answered for me.

I gave a little wave. 'Hello, I'm Gemma. I'm the new English teacher at St Bride's. I've just joined this term.'

The man got up from his stool and came out from behind the counter, holding out his hand to shake mine.

'Hello, I'm Hector.' He gave me another engaging smile. 'Well done on your new job. Such a gorgeous house and grounds to work in. If you need any help with book orders or book choices for the English department, I'm your man.'

He turned to Joe. 'You after your usual, Joe?'

Joe nodded and put a hand on my shoulder to guide me to the tearoom area at the back. Hector diverted to a door in the corner diagonally opposite the trade counter, presumably his stockroom. He opened it a fraction to call through it: 'Sophie! You've got tearoom customers!'

A pretty girl a little younger than me emerged and headed for the tearoom. Her forget-me-not blue eyes lit up when she saw Joe, who was positively glowing after our ride. She gave me a warm smile too.

As he settled himself at a tearoom table, the muscles in Joe's legs made the light metal chairs look spindly. Only then did I notice when he took off his waterproof jacket that beneath it he was wearing a Superman shirt.

14

CAFÉ CHAT

'Two cream teas, Joe?' said Sophie, bringing cups, saucers, spoons, plates, and a small jug of pouring cream to our table.

Joe raised his eyebrows at me for approval, and I nodded.

While she was fetching the teapot, I peered into the jug. 'Don't they do clotted cream with their cream teas?' I asked in a low voice, not wanting to seem rude. 'Or are we meant to pour this over our scones?'

Joe grinned. 'They do things a bit differently here. Taste it.'

He dipped the tip of his teaspoon into the jug, scooped up a tiny amount, then held it up for me to taste. As the cold liquid trickled into my mouth, my tongue curled involuntarily.

'Goodness, has it gone off?' I asked, shuddering and wiping my mouth with the back of my hand. Then a warm glow began to spread across my taste buds, and my face brightened. 'Oh wow, that's delicious.'

'It's just a little something Hector distils for his favourite customers,' Joe explained. 'But don't worry, we won't be downing it by the pint. You won't be too drunk to cycle safely home.'

Hector, watching us from the stool behind his counter, grinned and resumed his typing.

With our pot of tea came more cream, this time clotted, in a little stone pot, a plate of scones and a glass dish of home-made damson jam. The cups and saucers were emblazoned with the names of books and authors. On Joe's cup was Joseph Conrad's *The Secret Agent*, and on mine Virginia Woolf's *A Room of One's Own*.

As I drizzled purple jam across the cream on my scone, I noticed for the first time the soothing background music on the shop's sound system. Beethoven's Pastoral Symphony is one of my favourites. It had been too long since I'd last listened to classical music, Steven not being a fan.

Joe drank his first cup of tea quickly, topped mine up, then refilled his.

He called across to Hector, 'Gemma's doing herself down. She's not just the new English teacher, she's our new head of English.'

'Head of English in a department of one,' I corrected him. 'It's such a small school that each department has a staff of precisely one teacher.'

'Big fish in a small pond, hey?' Hector winked.

'More like a big fish in a toothglass.'

Hector laughed. 'I know what you mean. In my business, I'm director of sales, marketing, human resources, and finance. Plus I get to put out the dustbins. Don't I, Sophie?'

She nodded and smiled. 'He has his uses.'

Hector grinned. 'But I would be lost without her.'

Sophie's cheeks went pink. I wondered whether they were an item.

'Is there anything you'd like to ask Hector while we're here?' asked Joe, stirring more cream into his tea. 'Anything book related, I mean?'

'Or Sophie,' said Hector. 'Sophie's pretty knowledgeable about books these days.'

'Thanks, I think,' said Sophie.

I hesitated. I didn't want to reveal my lack of experience.

'Have you ever been in the school library, Hector?' I began.

'Sadly no,' he said. 'Other local schools invite me in to help update their libraries at least once a year. Schools' business helps keep our little shop afloat. But not St Bride's. I'm guessing you have a brilliant and inspired librarian who needs no help from me. Or perhaps she prefers to order online.'

I thought of Mavis steadfastly avoiding the internet.

'I don't think so,' I assured him. 'Judging by the state of the shelves and of my department's books, I suspect there's no budget. My class set of *A Midsummer Night's Dream* are priced in old money, predecimal.'

As I spoke, I realised this was further evidence of the school's financial difficulties. I should have known there'd be a catch with this job, which had until now seemed too good to be true. The organisation might even be on the brink of bankruptcy.

'So those books must be over fifty years old,' Hector was saying. 'I'm amazed they're still intact,'

'Doesn't say much for the girls' reading habits, does it?' said Joe.

'It might also be a space issue,' I said. 'The library shelves are pretty full, though mostly of vintage books that the girls don't use.'

'It's standard library practice to cull old disused books to make space for new,' Hector explained. 'And if any of the vintage ones are worth anything, she could sell them to fund new stock more appropriate for your pupils. I can help her with that, if she likes.'

'Do you deal in second-hand books too?'

Everything on the shop's shelves looked new.

'No, but I collect vintage curiosities as a hobby, so I know more about old books than the average high-street bookseller. In my flat upstairs, I've got a whole roomful. But I can hook her up with a friend in Oxford who would be happy to make her fair offers, if she's interested.'

I wasn't sure how Mavis would take to this intervention, but I wanted to keep on the right side of Hector.

'Thanks, that's very kind.'

He scribbled his friend's contact details on the back of one of the shop's promotional bookmarks and brought it over to me. After wiping my sticky fingers on a serviette, I picked it up and read it.

'But she knows him already,' I said, taken aback. 'That's the name and address I saw on a jiffy bag on her desk yesterday, before she turned it over. For some reason I don't think she wanted me to see it. But I'm very good at reading upside down, and quickly. That was the most useful thing I learned at school.'

Miss Harnett would be proud of me.

Hector bit back a smile. 'Perhaps she'd discovered a book in the old gentleman's library not fit for the eyes of your pupils and was sending it to him to get it out of their way. Jasper does buy books of that kind, among other things.'

I'd never thought of that.

'Mavis told me those top shelves are out of bounds for health and safety reasons. She never mentioned censorship.'

Joe took the bookmark from my hand to read the address. 'You'd better tell her she's been getting his postcode wrong.'

'You saw that envelope too?'

Joe hesitated. 'I'm Postman Joe, remember? Postlady, when the girls are about.' When Hector and Sophie exchanged knowing glances, I realised they were in on his act. 'More than one for this address. That's why I know the postcode by heart.'

It was Hector's turn to look surprised. 'That's funny. I'm sure Jasper would have mentioned it if he was regularly buying books from a school just up the road from me.'

Joe fidgeted a little. 'Maybe he doesn't realise.'

'But our postcodes are practically identical,' said Hector. 'He'd realise the school was nearby.'

'Who says Mavis is selling them to him anyway?' said Joe. 'He might just be borrowing them.'

When Joe looked away, Hector coughed, perhaps realising he'd touched on a sensitive point. Hector strolled over to the tearoom counter and lifted the glass dome to help himself to a piece of shortbread.

Joe changed the subject. 'So, Hector, how's that Land Rover of yours running?'

The ensuing explanation about gaskets and big ends went right over my head. I glanced at Sophie, who rolled her eyes, obviously feeling as excluded as I was. I moved to sit at the table nearest the counter so that we could chat.

Half an hour later, as Joe and I left the shop, replete with our cream teas, I heard Sophie say, 'Tell me, Hector, have you ever thought of taking up cycling?'

* * *

Riding back companionably side by side, we were halfway home before I had the confidence to tackle the issue of Mavis's secret profiteering. It would be easier to talk about here, where we could not be overheard by other staff or the girls.

'Joe, judging by all the gaps on the upper shelves, I'm guessing Mavis has been quietly disposing of school library books for some time.'

He was silent for a moment before he replied.

'Really, Gemma, it's none of my business, nor yours. As long as she pays me for the postage on her parcels, that's fine. And she always pays me straight away in cash from her own purse when I give her the receipt from the post office. It's not for me to know or care what's in the envelopes. It's not like she's asking me to be a drug runner, for goodness' sake. They're only books.'

'Yes, but they're the school's books. They're not hers to sell.'

He pursed his lips and pedalled a little faster, forcing me to gasp for breath to keep up with him. I hoped he wasn't about to sprint off and leave me behind.

'I'm not getting involved,' he called over his shoulder.

'Joe, you're not only involved, you're implicated. Doesn't that worry you?'

I didn't want him to get into trouble, but nor was I comfortable with watching the school's valuable books surreptitiously sold off at no profit to St Bride's when it needed every penny it could muster. Mavis's asset-stripping amounted to theft.

As we approached the lodge gates at the school entrance, he slowed down and waited for me to catch up.

'For all I know, she's giving all the money she makes to the bursar,' he said as we turned into the drive.

'Then how come she's paying you the postage out of her own purse?' I countered, cross with him for not supporting me. After all, he needed to keep the school afloat to protect himself just as much as I did. 'Do you think we should tell the bursar? From what Oriana's told me, the school could do with the extra income.'

Either Joe didn't hear my question or he ignored it, as we freewheeled the last few hundred metres down to the turning circle in front of the school. I trailed behind, applying my brakes on the slope, while Joe zoomed ahead unfettered, leaning into the rush of air. After we'd stowed our bikes in the cycle shed, Joe turned to me and fixed me with an appealing gaze.

'Look, Gemma, I know your intentions are good, but take it from me, it's best to let sleeping dogs lie on this one. It's not doing anyone any harm, is it? It's not like Mavis is beating the girls or doing anything illegal.'

He looked away before I could answer, making me wonder why he was so keen to cover for Mavis. Might she have something on him?

15

THE GOVERNORS' LUNCH

'Whatever you do, don't invite any of them back to your room.'

I didn't know why Oriana felt it necessary to repeat this warning as I left the staffroom to join the governors for lunch. I'd already sneaked a peek at them through the staffroom window as they parked their smart cars at the front of the house, and none of them looked a day under seventy. Not that age ever affected Steven's jealousy. He'd told me off for speaking to men of all ages, from a teenager to a nonagenarian.

I wondered why the governors had invited me to lunch. Nicolette had enlightened me over morning coffee.

'It is a thing all new staff must do.'

'What, like a job interview?'

My heart had sunk at the idea. More penetrating questions than Miss Harnett's might reveal my worthlessness as a teacher.

'*Mais non.* The governors, they just do this for show. They justify themselves. They want to look important to the school.'

Joe laid *The Times Educational Supplement* on the staffroom coffee table. 'And they've got time on their hands. They've all been pensioned off from plum city posts for years.' When Mavis flinched at the word 'pensioned', I wondered why. 'Pitching up here every so often gives them the illusion of power. Their wives just want them out from under their feet.'

The bursar brought his coffee over to join us. 'Their presence demonstrates the school is run efficiently and ethically and ensures our financial management is beyond reproach.'

'Compensates for your incompetence, you mean,' muttered Oriana without looking up from her marking.

My heart sank. Was the bursar's incompetence to blame for the school's current financial difficulties?

Mavis quietly moved towards the door and left the room.

That reminded me. 'I've been meaning to ask you, Bursar, how come the school's a registered charity when it's full of rich people?'

The bursar shook his head at my ignorance. 'According to the Charities Act, as a provider of education, we are a charitable institution. Charity status and the tax benefits it provides keep the wolf from the door. It makes all the difference between profit and loss. Sinking and swimming. Survival and decline. Flying—'

Oriana snapped her final marked exercise book shut and threw down her pen. 'I wondered what had happened to the staffroom thesaurus. The bursar must have swallowed it.' She got up to return her empty coffee cup to the trolley.

The bursar smiled feebly, as if trying to pass her remark off as a compliment. 'So you see, Gemma, the governors come here once a term to review matters with the head, and with me, and with any other staff who request to see them, and to welcome our newest employees. Plus of course it gives us ample opportunity to, ah, hint to them of any impending financial requirements not met by fee income. They are all men of means, and it's important to keep them on side. Many a time they've dipped their hands into their own pockets to top up our funds or bankroll an urgent project.'

'I'm not sure I have anything of interest to say to them yet. Couldn't I see them once I've been here a bit longer? Perhaps after half-term?'

The bursar waved a hand dismissively. 'Oh no, what they say goes. Besides, they like to come early in the term to get the best lunch, while Rosemary's still in a good mood.'

He'd wandered away to retrieve a packet of biscuits from his pigeonhole.

'The girls, they love the school sausages, but the governors, they do not,' Nicolette had explained with a twinkle in her eye. 'They are not at all like French sausages. *Ah, le beau Toulousain!* Now that's what I call a *saucisson!*'

* * *

When I arrived at the appointed time at the head's private dining room, part of the suite attached to her study, she and the bursar were sitting at opposite ends of a long table. They looked like lord and lady of the manor hosting a society lunch. If Miss Harnett were absent, it could have passed for the dining room of a traditional gentlemen's club. I wondered whether the governors had a secret handshake.

At each side of the table sat three elderly gentlemen in

business suits and regimental ties, a couple of them with starched linen napkins tucked into their collars. The array of cutlery before us heralded five courses, and the trio of glasses a range of wines. I hadn't expected to see wine on the table at a school function, and I determined to stick to water to keep my wits about me.

To my embarrassment, all the men except the bursar stood up as I entered the room. He shuffled to his feet when he realised he'd been left behind. One governor chivalrously pulled out the only empty chair for me with a kindly, genuine smile. I hoped the smell of mothballs emanating from his beautifully tailored dark-blue suit would not taint the taste of the food.

As I sat down, everyone else resumed their seats.

'May I introduce Miss Lamb, our new head of English,' said Miss Harnett, holding one hand out to me.

I wanted to say, 'Please call me Gemma,' but feared breaching their etiquette. I didn't want to risk even the slightest upset that might jeopardise their financial support for the school. They might be St Bride's last chance of survival – and mine and Joe's of retaining our secret hideaway.

Miss Harnett continued, 'Miss Lamb, I am delighted to introduce you to our governing body. St Bride's is blessed with governors from all walks of life, bringing a wealth of perspectives to our decision-making. They are a wise executive and we are lucky to have them.'

Miss Harnett paused to bestow a beatific smile upon each governor in turn. She knew how to work a room. As the elderly gentlemen, all at least twenty years older than her, basked in the warmth of her gaze, I realised that to them she must have seemed relatively young and lovely. In her youth, she must have been a stunning beauty as well as a spirited companion.

I glanced at the bursar to see how he was responding to her performance, which he must have witnessed many times. His tight, unmoving smile suggested his teeth were gritted beneath it. Whatever this queen and her courtiers decided about the management of the school estate, it was down to him to implement it and to make ends meet financially, within the tight legal constraints placed upon a registered charity in a heritage building. I almost felt sorry for him, until I remembered Oriana's remark about his incompetence.

There was a light tap on the door, which swung open gently to admit nine of the youngest pupils. Each bore a plate of pastry tartlets nestling on a bed of frisée lettuce. A particular girl was assigned to each of us for the duration of the meal, and they returned at intervals to remove the remnants of the previous course and replace it with the next. I wondered whether their role was punishment or reward.

Nicolette told me afterwards that being picked for waitress duty was a prized treat, because each girl was allowed to eat the leftovers. Too nervous to eat much of my lunch, I was glad my waitress would have enjoyed the rest of it.

As the courses came and went, to the accompaniment of the occasional suppressed belch and contented sigh from the menfolk, the governors took it in turns to introduce themselves to me, along with their area of responsibility on the board. As the first of them began, I wondered how on earth I'd remember them all, until Lewis Carroll came to my rescue.

Finance was the realm of the Mad Hatter, who might just

as well have been wearing a top hat priced 10/6, so clear were the pound signs in his eyes. Expensively dressed, he sported a large black onyx signet ring on his right hand and a chunky gold one on his left. His red and blue striped tie was anchored in place by a magnificent pearl.

The welfare officer was the dormouse, pink scalp covered with flat sandy hair as neat as a small rodent's fur. He kept nodding off, well-manicured hands clasped contentedly across the velvet waistcoat constraining his round stomach. The girl looking after him got his measure early on, going out of her way to clatter his dishes when setting down each new course so he didn't sleep through it.

Responsibility for curriculum and careers lay with the Red King. He seemed to take himself seriously, even if no one else did, least of all Miss Harnett, who contradicted nearly every statement he made.

The sprightly old gentleman with long white whiskers could only be the March Hare. Full of energy not always well directed, he sent his wineglass flying twice. Flinging his arms out to emphasise a point about the dangers of polished stair-cases, he instigated a hailstorm of green peas from a serving dish about to be set on the table. His area of interest was health and safety.

Matching the remaining governors with the fictional characters so familiar to me, I relaxed enough to enjoy the stories that followed their introductions. If the conversation stalled, the headmistress gently prompted one or the other to share a particular anecdote. Each looked delighted to be asked.

They must all have heard each other's tales many times before but they likely felt it a small price to pay for the succession of delicious dishes which we steadily absorbed. It was excellent food, dazzlingly presented, a welcome interlude for Rosemary between serving a hundred identical covers of cottage pie or spag bol day after day.

By the time coffee came around, I felt stuffed, even though I'd eaten barely a quarter of each serving. How the governors, who had also put away plenty of wine, could now be expected to do school business was beyond me. Thankfully, as the empty coffee cups were taken away, Miss Harnett made it clear that I had done all that was expected of me.

'Miss Lamb, it has been a delight to have your company, but it's time for us to move on to corporate business which need not concern you. You may be excused.' Her eyes twinkled mischievously. 'You'll be just in time for afternoon tea.'

As I stood up, she turned to the bursar. 'Geoffrey, if you'd kindly fetch what needs signing, we will proceed.'

This was just as well, as the Red King was now sleeping as soundly as the dormouse. Like Alice at the Mad Hatter's tea party, I was glad to make my escape.

* * *

'What surprised me most,' I confided in Nicolette when we had the staffroom to ourselves, 'is that the headmistress seems to govern the governors rather than the other way around. Surely that can't be right?'

Nicolette gave a wide, indulgent smile. 'Ah, these poor old men do not stand a chance against her. Miss Harnett can ask you to do something that you do not want to do, but she makes you glad to do it for her. These old men may be called governors, but it is Miss Harnett who is in charge.'

The door opened to admit Oriana, a pile of exercise books balanced elegantly on her outstretched palm.

'Survived the governors' lunch intact, Gemma?' she asked.

She began raiding the stationery cupboard for pens.

'Yes, thanks. You were right, Nicolette, they didn't ask me any difficult questions. Actually they all seemed rather sweet old men.'

I couldn't understand Oriana's constant warning against their seductive powers, nor could I believe that an illicit liaison with one of them had been responsible for poor mysterious Caroline's downfall. The only reason I could imagine any of them wanting to find their way into my bedroom would be to enjoy a restorative postprandial nap.

Oriana narrowed her eyes.

'Don't let them fool you for a moment. They've got all the charisma of boa constrictors. Rich boa constrictors, too, and deadly ones! Governors! They're all beasts: a special species of beast all of their own.'

I resolved to remain alert for whatever strange danger she was alluding to and chastised myself for too easily dropping my guard under their spell.

16

THE MOTHER OF REINVENTION

I was just enjoying my breakfast the next morning, listening to a lively group of girls explaining the details of their favourite hairstyle of the moment – a complex system of four plaits woven together across the back of the head – when Oriana appeared at the door and sauntered across to take her usual place at the head of her nearby table without even looking at me. I wondered whether I'd done something to offend her.

'Speaking of hairstyles, Miss Blister's done it again,' said one of the girls on my table.

The other girls followed her gaze, giving me licence to scrutinise her too. Oriana's attention was fixed on her coffee. If she knew we were staring at her, she was doing a good job of ignoring us.

It wasn't just her hair that had changed, dark brown curls replacing her previous jet-black lob, but her make-up too. Gone was the dramatic black eyeliner and perfectly applied lipstick. In its place was a much softer look: velvety skin glowing beneath peachy foundation, her soft cheeks pink and her lips rosy. Her eyebrows, only the day before as black as coal, were now light brown above eyes made wider with skilful application of blue mascara and pale pink eyeshadow. Even her eyes had changed colour: chocolate brown yesterday, silvery blue today.

'I suppose that means Mr Aziz didn't fall for her after all,' declared Amelia, one of the older girls on the next table. 'That's her Mrs Aziz phase cut short.'

'Another man who's slipped through her fingers,' said Madalen.

A scraping of chairs from the table behind us made me realise my girls were eating at too leisurely a pace.

'Chop-chop, girls, or you'll be late for your next lesson.'

'Chop-chop, miss? That's a funny saying. Do you mean like karate chops or pork chops?'

'Or lamb. Miss Lamb should prefer lamb.'

'No, that would make her a cannibal.'

The younger girls fell about laughing, except for the vegetarians among them who clapped their hands over their mouths in horror.

'Never mind the semantics,' I said, impressing myself with the kind of word an English teacher ought to use, and making a mental note to look up the origins of 'chop-chop' in the dictionary in case any of them asked me later. 'Let's finish our breakfast and get on with our day.'

As I swallowed the rest of my coffee, I was thankful that none of the girls had noticed what was blatantly obvious to me: that Oriana Bliss had morphed overnight into a more beautiful and better-groomed version of me.

* * *

When Oriana entered the staffroom at morning break, I
noticed other staff exchange knowing looks in between
stealing glances at the pair of us. Mavis locked eyes with me in
quiet complicity and edged closer on the window seat.

'Take no notice, Gemma. You know what they say about
imitation.'

I tried to look unconcerned, but I didn't fool her.

'Don't worry,' she said, patting my arm. 'She doesn't mean
anything by it, despite demonstrating a deep-rooted complex
about who on earth she actually is.'

Joe got up from his usual armchair to join us.

'What are you saying, Mavis? Of course she means something by it.' There was a glint of amusement in his eyes.

Oriana collected a note from her pigeonhole and flounced
out of the staffroom without stopping for coffee.

'So is that her natural look?' I asked after the door had
closed behind her.

Joe shrugged. 'You'd need to be David Attenborough to
catch that rare a sighting.'

Mavis set her empty cup and saucer on the window seat
and folded her arms.

'No need for sour grapes, Joe.' She turned to me. 'When
Joe first joined the staff, Oriana was all Lycra sportswear and
aerodynamic hair.'

Joe had the decency to look slightly abashed.

'He's just miffed because she dropped him like a hot tyre
iron,' Mavis went on, 'as soon as she realised he wasn't as rich

and famous as her usual prey, despite his array of fancy bicycles.'

'The Rolls Royces of bicycles,' Joe said proudly. 'But it's probably just as well. Imagine going out with someone like that long-term. It would be exhausting, like dating ten girls at once and never knowing which one was going to turn up.'

'You're very forgiving, Joe,' said Mavis, getting to her feet to return her empty cup to the tea trolley. She took mine from my hands as she passed. 'Considering all she ever does is jettison men like you from her life.'

'Only if they don't drop her first,' said Joe. 'Let's hope she never tries it on with any of the Russian girls' dads. The odds are that some of them must be secret agents. If they drive cars like James Bond's, she may one day find herself modelling their ejector seat.'

Mavis sighed and headed for the door. Joe took the space she'd vacated beside me, straightening his pleated lacrosse skirt over his cycle shorts as he made himself comfortable.

'Never mind, Gemma, at least Oriana's chosen a decent role model for a change.'

I touched my own dark brown curls and realised I should have done a better job of brushing them before breakfast. It was too bad to have someone better at being you than you were yourself.

'What on earth makes you think she'd pick me as a role model?' I asked. 'She's naturally so much more elegant and beautiful.'

Joe raised his eyebrows.

'Don't sell yourself short, Gemma. Not everyone likes the highly made-up look.'

I couldn't help but smile back in gratitude, despite wondering who she was hoping to attract by looking like me.

'Does Oriana really hit on all the single dads?' I asked.

'Yes, but not all at once. She only needs one as her get-out-of-jail-free card. I don't know whether you've twigged yet, but having St Bride's on your CV isn't exactly a passport to better jobs elsewhere. If St Bride's ever goes down the pan, so do our careers.'

And so does our safe accommodation, I added in my head.

At his allusion to St Bride's financial plight, Mavis got to her feet and shuffled over to check her pigeonhole.

'Don't mind Mavis,' said Joe in a low voice. 'She's only jealous that she can't escape the same way as Oriana might.'

'But she doesn't really have to worry about that, does she? I don't suppose Mavis has long to go until she retires, and she'll have her pension to support her.'

Joe pursed his lips. 'Technically, she's past retirement age. But her age is irrelevant, because she's got no home beyond St Bride's, and only a state pension. She's only been here a few years. Miss Harnett took pity on her after her last school went bust, and her private pension with it. She'd spent her entire career there until then. Leaving St Bride's will spell penury for her. The only way she wants to leave is in a box.'

'In a box? What, you mean she'll post herself somewhere? Even Cycleman will have trouble getting a box that big on the back of his bike. Unless you've got a trailer you're not telling me about?'

He flexed his arm muscles and grinned.

I checked the wall clock. Any minute now, the bell would ring for the next lesson. I followed Joe to the door where we parted company, Joe heading to the lacrosse pitch and I to the classroom quad.

On the way, I made a mental note to ask the bursar with my fingers firmly crossed about joining the school pension scheme as soon as I'd passed my probationary period. Then I fell to wondering why Oriana took such an old-fashioned approach to dating for someone so feisty. If she wanted to get rich, why didn't she just change career sector instead of selling her soul to a millionaire? She was quick-witted and capable, and, as head of maths, highly numerate. I could picture her making a killing as a City trader. She should be more daring, more independent.

As should I. Pot, kettle.

It was only as I arrived at my classroom door that I realised there must be something special keeping Oriana at St Bride's. Not a pension crisis, like Mavis. But what?

17

CUPBOARD LOVE

The kinder Mavis was to me, the more uncomfortable I felt about suspecting her of defrauding the school with her secret book sales. Now that I knew she was in financial difficulties, it seemed more likely that she was guilty, but I still didn't want to believe it.

Then it struck me. With a little research, I might prove her innocence. Then I could relax and enjoy our growing friendship with a clear conscience. It might have been that those dusty old books were worthless, and she was doing the school a favour by disposing of them.

The bursar could verify their value. Oriana had told me he was in the habit of selling the family silver. If any books in the library were valuable, he'd have sold them off long ago. What could be simpler than asking him?

During a free period mid-afternoon, I knocked on the bursar's door, my strategy at the ready.

'Come,' called the bursar from within.

As I opened the door, he chucked a glowing cigar butt into

the fireplace, where it landed lit side up and burned out before it could ignite the papers in the grate. Seated in an antique leather swivel chair built for a much taller man, he beckoned me to the low, rush-seated visitor's chair facing him. We were the same height standing up, but when I sat down I had to look up to him. A classic short person's power game. I wondered what sort of visitor's chair Napoleon had in his campaign tent. I'd ask Judith Gosling later.

A cool breeze from the open window stirred the door behind me, which I hadn't shut properly. The bursar glanced at it but said nothing, perhaps hoping I'd soon be closing it properly myself from the other side.

I tried not to pay too much attention to the ten neat stacks of papers that completely covered the top of his antique double-pedestal desk. I wondered where he actually did any work until he pulled out a small wooden flap from beneath the desktop, placed a shorthand pad on it, and took a gold propelling pencil from a pot made out of some poor animal's hoof. I wondered whether the hoof had belonged to one of the creatures whose heads were stuffed and mounted on plaques on the walls above us – exotic, moth-eaten trophies of Victorian colonial hunters. I shuddered. How could anyone be comfortable working surrounded by stuffed dead animals?

The bursar locked his eyes on me. 'How can I help you, Gemma?'

I took a deep breath.

'I wanted to ask you a technical question about the school library.'

'Can't Miss Brook help you?'

'To be honest, I haven't asked her. I thought you'd be more expert on this particular point.'

Smiling at the flattery, he sat back in his big chair, elbows stretched out to reach its wooden armrests, which were shiny with wear, and pressed his fingertips together across his lap.

I'd planned my pitch carefully.

'You see, I'm developing a project for my Y7 class about the history of books and printing, from scrolls and clay tablets through to e-books and audiobooks.'

He nodded, comfortable so far.

'I thought I'd conclude with a lesson in making their own books using traditional bookbinding methods. You know, folding and stitching paper, gluing on boards and endpapers. I was planning to borrow some of the older books from the top shelves in the library to demonstrate those techniques. The books the girls use from the lower shelves are all machine-made.'

His brow creased and he gazed out of the window. Now the flattery had stopped, he looked plain bored.

'Your lesson plans are nothing to do with me, Gemma, provided there are no parental complaints. Just keep supplying the goods so the parents pay the bills. That's all I ask of you.'

I nodded. 'Of course. It's just that I was wondering whether there are any old books in the library that I shouldn't touch. You know, the kind of rare collectibles that may only be handled by the librarian with white cotton gloves.'

He peeled his hands apart to examine his fingernails, as if wondering whether he'd give himself clearance to handle such treasures.

'No, there's nothing valuable there,' he said with authority. 'What is vintage to us was contemporary and commonplace to Lord Bunting. Just being old doesn't make it valuable.'

'Are you sure there are no rare first editions, for example? Or older books from earlier times? Many rich gentlemen used to collect old books and manuscripts for their country house libraries.' I wanted to say incunabula, a word I'd first come across in Lord Peter Wimsey novels, but I was unsure how to pronounce it.

'Not Lord Bunting,' said the bursar. 'He was more of an outdoor type.' He gazed fondly at the tiger's head over the fireplace with the same expression that Miss Harnett reserved for McPhee. 'A hunting, shooting, fishing man. A real man's man.'

If the bursar was right about the books, Mavis was innocent, which made me glad, although I was sad for the tiger.

'That's not surprising considering how long he must have spent underground developing his patent tunnelling equipment,' I replied. 'He must have been keen to get out into the fresh air.'

I looked around me for a moment. 'Did this used to be Lord Bunting's study?' I asked.

The bursar nodded, beaming, and in that moment I realised that when not overshadowed by Miss Harnett, he fancied himself as Bunting's natural successor: a latter-day lord of the manor, controlling the estate's finances as Lord Bunting must once have done.

But I hadn't come here for a history lesson, so I brought the conversation back on track. 'So it doesn't matter which books I use for my project?'

He shook his head. 'No, you can take the lot of them for all

I care. That would save the domestic staff a bit of dusting. Just run them past Miss Brook first to be sure she has no other plans for them. And be careful as you fetch them down from the upper shelves. I live in fear that one day someone will topple down those library steps and sue the school for damages. I've been in two minds as to whether to remove them altogether on grounds of health and safety.'

He got up and strolled round to the fireplace, fishing out of a vast wicker basket a yellowing leather-bound volume whose cover was falling apart. The binding looked far too thick for the sparse contents. When he flipped it open, I realised why.

'If it helps the girls to see a book dissected, feel free to cut them up. The books, I mean, not the girls, ha ha.'

I shuddered.

'Here's one to start you off. I found it lying on the floor in the library the other day with nearly all its colour plates missing, and I've been using its remaining pages as firelighters ever since.' He slammed the book shut, issuing a small cloud of papery dust. 'Honestly, you'd think whatever child had done that could have taken the trouble to put the rest of the book in the bin. Our girls aren't usually untidy. The housemistresses have trained them well.'

I took the proffered book from his hands, crumbs of leather like finely tilled soil falling into my lap. Alarm bells were starting to ring in my head. Might Mavis be selling the colour plates to framers?

'What makes you think it was a pupil who cut the pictures out?'

The bursar sighed as if I was dense.

'The girls are allowed to decorate the walls of their dorms

with posters and photos. This particular girl must have taken a liking to whatever pictures were in this book. She wrecked it, but if it keeps her happy and her father paying her fees, I'm not going to make an issue of it. Believe me, Gemma, we can't afford to lose any more fee income.'

He sat down again at his desk, returning his fingers to the steeple position.

'Okay, thanks, bursar. I'll tell Mavis I've cleared it with you before I start. And don't worry about health and safety. I know the steps are out of bounds for the girls. I'll be the only one to use them.'

A draught from the open window whistled around my shoulders, rattling the door behind me. I fastened the buttons on my cardigan, then got up from my seat, clutching the vandalised book to my chest.

'I'll make a start straight away.'

The bursar nodded, as if dismissing a servant, his mind already on whatever was next on his agenda. As I turned to leave, he was crossing to a tall cupboard that filled the alcove behind him from floor to ceiling. I hoped it didn't contain more stuffed animals.

Just outside his study door, I realised I'd left my book bag by my chair, so I gave a cursory tap to indicate my return before darting in to retrieve it.

'Sorry, just forgot my bag,' I said, quickly seizing it and retreating, but not before I'd had time to notice the bursar swivel round from the open cupboard to stare at me in horror. Pinned to the inside of the cupboard doors was an array of pictures that covered every inch of the ancient oak. For a split second, I thought they might be the images he'd cut out of an old book out of bounds to the girls. Victorian pornography, perhaps?

But no, every image was a modern colour photograph of a woman fully dressed in a multitude of styles and costumes, and all were unmistakably of the same person: the poised and imperious Oriana Bliss. This was the bursar's secret shrine to her.

18

COOKING THE BOOKS

Knowing that Mavis was currently teaching a geography lesson, I stumbled back to the library to investigate further, trying to put the bursar's secret out of my mind.

I lay his dissected book on a library table and began to flick through it. Just three coloured plates, each ripped, were left: painstakingly drawn botanical illustrations, almost photographic in their accuracy. I couldn't believe they'd be the decoration of choice for a teenager's bedroom... but I could imagine Mavis selling them to a picture dealer. I'd seen market stalls with boxes and boxes of prints like this, set into cardboard mounts and polybags, selling at the kind of price I'd expect to pay for something already framed. I'd even bought one myself once, a print from a vintage copy of *Pride and Prejudice*, as a souvenir of a Jane Austen pilgrimage I'd made to Bath with my mum, just before I'd met Steven.

I flipped to the index of illustrations to check how many the complete book would have held. A hundred and forty-seven. Even if Mavis had made only a fiver on each print, she'd have made a significant profit from just this book.

I flipped back to the title page, relieved to see it wasn't a first edition. I noted its title, author, and publisher on my phone, before leaving the remains of the book casually on a side table to see what happened to it. If Mavis was guilty of selling the plates for her own profit, she'd sneak it away and destroy it to hide the evidence. On the other hand, if it really was the work of the girls, she would blame them and most likely be angry. Next period she was due to supervise prep in the library. I wouldn't have to wait long to see which it would be.

Just as I was leaving the book in its conspicuous spot on the table, Mavis entered the library, back earlier than I'd expected. Perhaps I'd misread her timetable.

'Ah, I've been looking for that!' she exclaimed, sweeping the book up into her arms. 'One of the cleaners must have moved it.' She pressed it to her chest. 'You'd better dash, Gemma, or you'll be late for your next lesson. Hairnet hates lateness. It's one of the few things that makes her really cross.'

Not half as cross as finding out someone had been vandalising school property for their own gain might make her, I thought, but I smiled sweetly and trotted off to class.

I had to wait till the end of my next lesson to look up the value of the disembowelled book. Searching online in the privacy of my empty classroom, I found it listed on several antiquarian bookshop sites. The estimated sale price of the whole book was only £20, but single plates cut from it were on sale for that much each. Dismantling the book and selling them separately therefore represented sound business practice. The plates would be cheaper to post, too, without the heavy leather binding.

Now I came to think of it, if she was doing anything surreptitious, why would she ask Joe to post the books at all? She could just take the books to the post office herself on her days off. Although working in a boarding school was full on, especially for housemistresses, all the staff got one weekday afternoon off every week, and every fourth weekend was free when the girls went home for an exeat. She had plenty of opportunity to post parcels herself.

Unless she was confident that Joe wouldn't guess or ask about the contents of her packages... that was a non-starter, as the addresses would give her game away. They'd all be antiquarian or second-hand bookshops. It wasn't as if Joe couldn't read.

But... that was the only explanation I could think of for why Joe wouldn't latch on to Mavis's game. I nurtured this strange fantasy for a moment, scrabbling for supporting evidence. When we'd visited the bookshop in Wendlebury Barrow, he hadn't so much as glanced at a book, never mind bought one. But no, that was too fanciful for words. Surely no one could function as a PE teacher without being able to read or write? On the other hand, if he could pull off posing as a woman when he so obviously wasn't...

With relief I remembered Joe had pointed out that Mavis was using the wrong postcode for Hector's friend's bookshop. And he was always perusing the jobs section in *The Times Educational Supplement* in the staffroom. Perhaps spending so

much time cloistered away at St Bride's was making me lose
touch with reality.

As the last one to leave the staffroom the following afternoon,
I had just set my empty cup and saucer on the tea trolley and
was about to walk past the staff pigeonholes to get to the door.
These quaint old wooden boxes were either empty or barely
used, as these days most school correspondence was done by
email, but in the early years of the school, they must have been
the focal point of communication with the outside world. I'd
noticed similar sets of pigeonholes in the corridors by the
dormitories, each array of twenty-five wooden boxes meticu-
lously handcrafted decades before by the school's resident
handyman. What excitement the contents must have caused
the girls before the advent of mobile phones.

Now staff pigeonholes tended to be used more for online
shopping deliveries (there was a large table beneath for
anything that wouldn't fit), or for memos between teachers,
hastily scribbled by hand between lessons. Some teachers
used them to store packets of sweets or biscuits for a quick
energy burst between lessons, or spare pens and pencils to
save them bringing pencil cases from their classrooms.

Only one pigeonhole jumped out at me now as being used
for its original purpose of storing post. That was Mavis
Brook's. Three Manilla envelopes lay unopened, each
addressed in fountain pen and stamped rather than franked.
One of them had the name and logo of Hector's friend's bookshop in Oxford embossed on its top-left corner.

I glanced around to make sure no one was there to see me before slipping it between the pages of the register I happened to have under my arm. Inwardly I thanked Miss Harnett for giving me the idea of what to do next in my quest to prove Mavis's innocence.

19

FULL STEAM AHEAD

Although I'd not had the benefit of Miss Harnett's privileged prep school education, I did have one advantage as a child that she'd lacked: access to YouTube. Opening my laptop and searching for 'how to steam open an envelope', I soon discovered there was more to it than simply holding it over a boiling kettle. I also learned how to reseal it to leave your intervention undetected.

An eager young woman vlogger demonstrated how to use a steam iron in place of a kettle. If an envelope proved particularly recalcitrant, she'd also slip a razor blade under the flap. A middle-aged scientist type showed how putting an envelope in the deep freezer for a couple of hours caused sufficient chemical change in the glue to destroy its adhesive properties, as did twelve seconds in the microwave in case of more urgent need.

Each of the YouTubers insisted they were doing this just for fun, or with virtuous intent such as having forgotten to place a cheque inside a letter before sealing it. Licking the gummed strip, explained the scientist, reactivates the original glue, provided you can bear the thought of putting your tongue where a stranger's has been.

My flat's kitchenette lacked a freezer, but it did contain a microwave and a kettle. Twelve seconds later, I was holding the hot open envelope with a tea towel to prevent scalding, and extracting a compliment slip with my eyebrow tweezers to avoid leaving fresh fingerprints. Attached to the compliment slip was a cheque for £20 payable to Miss M. Brook. A book title and author's name were handwritten on the compliment slip. It seemed this particular bookseller – or in this case book buyer – shared Mavis's aversion for modern technology. Which was handy for me, because if they'd paid her online by bank transfer, I wouldn't have had this evidence in my hand.

For a moment I stared at the cheque in disbelief, before seizing my phone and snapping a photo of both it and the comp slip. Then I slid them back into the envelope, licked the tip of my finger, ran it along the gummed flap and pressed it closed. Only too late did I realise I'd resealed it with my DNA, but the letter still looked virgin, so I hoped that no one would ever think of testing it.

Feeling drained, I slumped down on my sofa and set the envelope on the seat beside me. As I took in the significance of my discovery, I wondered what to do next.

Sounds of girls returning from lessons started to echo along the corridor, so I jumped up, slipped the letter back inside my register, and darted down the stairs. It was important to sneak it back into Mavis's pigeonhole before she might detect its absence.

But what I should do in the longer term about her activity completely eluded me. If this was a one-off sale, a mere £20 was insignificant in the scheme of things. But was this the exception to a flurry of much higher value cheques, or only the closest she'd come yet to hitting the jackpot, which was not that close? To give her the benefit of the doubt, it might not have been for the sale of a library book at all, but for one of her own. That seemed unlikely, given how many gaps there were on the upper shelves in the library.

No, I was becoming increasingly certain that this was an ongoing exercise, a steady drip-feed of school property to the outside world for the benefit of Mavis's pocket. I wondered how on earth to put a stop to it, and to stem the draining of the school's assets, without seeming a sneak or a busybody, and losing the respect of the rest of the staff. And who could I trust to help me?

20

DORM PATROL

I had no further leisure time that evening to consider how to
tackle Mavis's secret as it was the one night of the week when I
was on duty for pastoral care. As well as having an afternoon
off each weekday, every housemistress had one evening off, on
which she was free to leave school after supper and return
before midnight. Her dormitory duties for that evening were
assigned to another member of staff, and in Oriana's case, this
was me.

Before she left, she briefed me on my responsibilities,
which sounded straightforward, provided the girls cooper-
ated. Until supper, I'd have to supervise an hour's prep, during
which I could do some marking. After they'd eaten, the girls
were allowed to socialise within their house, in their dorms or
in their common room. They might watch television or a
DVD suitable for their age group, play games, or simply sit
and chat. At 8.45 p.m., the bedtime warning bell would alert
them to get ready for bed, and by 9 p.m. the younger girls
should be in bed. For the older girls, everything was an hour

later. So quiet reading was allowed until 9.30 p.m., or 10.30 p.m. for the older set. Smartphones were allowed only between supper and the bedtime bell, and only for messages home. Phones, tablets, and e-readers on airplane settings were allowed for bedtime reading, but most girls preferred printed books.

The timetable sounded very civilised to me, emulating how one might spend an idyllic family evening at home in the days before high-tech devices and media streaming split families into parallel and isolated online activities . I suspected that was Miss Harnett's plan.

I was to turn the lights off after each age group's allotted reading time, and after that I was free to go back to my flat. In the case of an emergency, the girls were allowed to knock on my door any time before midnight, the official end of the evening off, when the housemistress, like Cinderella, had to be back in school in a fit state to resume her duties.

Oriana gave me a quick tour of the Poorhouse dormitories and acquainted me with the minutiae of the rules about tidiness, showers, and so on.

'By the way,' she added lightly as we left the fifth and final dorm, 'have you completely finished with Steven?'

Her question startled me, and I forced a smile.

'You make me sound like a cat playing with a mouse.'

She looked away. 'I mean, do you consider your relationship over? You're not just taking a break during term time? You don't seem the type to be in an open relationship.'

'No. No, you're right about that. It's definitely over. Why do you ask?'

And then it dawned on me. She was interested in him for

herself. That's why her latest makeover was essentially an impression of me.

Oriana flashed me a tight smile and slipped on the elegant, dark, wool coat that she'd been carrying over her arm. It was a more expensive, better-quality version of my own winter coat. 'Good. I just wanted to be sure. I hope I haven't upset you by asking. You see, when I fended him off for you, he gave me his card and asked me to call him.'

I shook my head, appalled by how quickly he'd got over our break-up. 'No, of course not. That's fine. I'm fine with that in principle. Only are you sure it's what you want? I mean, I'm not sure he's really your type.'

Actually, I don't think a controlling bully is anyone's type.

Oriana tutted.

'Gemma, I'm sure you have the best intentions, but you don't really know me well enough yet to be able to make a judgement call like that. Believe me, I know men, and I know what I'm doing.'

Before I could elaborate, she turned and marched away from me towards the marble staircase and headed for the front door.

With some time to spare before I needed to make my dorm patrol, I headed for the narrower stairs used by the girls to avoid her realising I was shadowing Oriana, and dashed to the staffroom just in time to see a familiar red car sweeping up to the school. As it emerged from behind the foliage on to the last stretch of the drive, I realised it was as I feared: Steven had come to collect her. Only then did I see that I'd missed my opportunity to ask Max to exclude Steven from the school grounds, way back when I'd first met him and he'd asked me whether I had any security issues. I'd wasted a second chance, too, when I bumped into him alone in the mausoleum.

Standing back from the window in the hope that Steven wouldn't see me, I watched, wide-eyed, as Oriana opened the passenger door, stepped in, and leaned over to kiss him on both cheeks before strapping on her safety belt. The car, being electric, was silent as it moved off, apart from the crunching of gravel beneath its tyres.

I felt like an actress watching her understudy take over her role – a role I was glad to be shot of and one I knew she wouldn't really want. Was this a one-night only substitution or a permanent role? Steven might have an important corporate dinner to attend, as he often did, to which he'd agreed to bring me before realising I'd left him. I could imagine him fielding Oriana, rather than lose face with his bosses or clients by having to tell them I'd done a bunk. Steven liked to appear to be in charge.

But then so did Oriana. Perhaps that made her a better match for him than I was – a new, improved, more confident and dynamic version of me, similar only in appearance. I remembered noticing the low-cut top she had changed into for her evening out. If I'd worn that, Steven would have scolded me for making myself look cheap or throwing myself at other men. On Oriana, he might just find it sexy.

Oriana was all that I wasn't: assertive, strong-willed, self-assured. I couldn't see her putting up with Steven's possessiveness or his angry outbursts when she did something wrong. But I still wanted to warn her about them in case she was planning to see him again, and I needed to find a way to do that without sounding bitter or jealous.

On the other hand, perhaps I'd brought out the worst in him. With Oriana, he might be a different person altogether. He'd always told me it was my fault when anything went wrong between us, and for a long time I had believed him. But now that I'd spent some time away from him, in the safety of St Bride's, I wasn't so sure.

I closed my eyes and covered them with my hands, unsure what the feelings roiling about in my belly signified: relief, envy, jealousy, remorse, longing, love, worry? Or it might have been too much school coffee.

The tolling of the school bell made me open my eyes. It was 7 p.m. For now, I had other things to worry about. I'd warn Oriana tomorrow. I returned my empty cup and saucer to the trolley, slipped out of the staffroom, and headed for the polished staircase for the start of prep in the Poorhouse.

21

STORY TIME

As I turned down the corridor, I wondered whether I had what it takes to be a housemistress. And just what did it take anyway? Having never been to boarding school myself, before I came to St Bride's I had only a hazy idea of what the role required. Now I was here, I noted that it didn't seem designed for a particular personality, judging from the quartet of housemistresses at St Brides. Each was so different that you'd be hard-pressed to find any common qualities between them: Oriana was haughty, self-contained, controlled; Nicolette was warm, organised, calm; Mavis was terse, old-fashioned, but caring beneath her shell; Judith Gosling was matter-of-fact and wry. How did Miss Harnett decide who to appoint?

As I took my place at the desk in the Poorhouse prep room with a pile of essays to mark, I was glad that Oriana had made my duties tonight so clear. As a quiet, discreet presence, I should keep order without intruding on the girls' leisure time or private conversations.

At 8 p.m., two of the girls helped me to make twenty-five

mugs of cocoa and hand them round with a huge biscuit tin. We all enjoyed watching an absorbing nature programme about wombats, with much oohing and aahing, followed by earnest enquiries about the possibility of keeping a wombat as a House pet.

I broke the news to them gently.

'I don't think there are any wombats in England.'

'Yes, there are, miss, I've seen them at Longleat,' said Imogen.

'No, they're lions, silly,' said Tilly. 'I've seen the signs for them on the motorway nearby.'

'They haven't only got lions,' said Imogen. 'They've got loads of animals. They've got tigers and elephants and monkeys and everything. And now wombats and koala bears.'

'When we went there, we went on the safari park drive-through and a monkey sat on my dad's car and did a massive poo,' said Poppy. 'It was worth going just for that.'

I looked at my watch. 'Speaking of dads, isn't it time any of you who want to message home did so?'

Imogen let out a joyful peal of laughter. 'I thought you were going to say "speaking of massive poos".'

The others collapsed into giggles as they reached for their phones. I couldn't imagine Oriana leading a conversation like this. I hoped it wouldn't feature in their texts and emails home.

I expected to have trouble getting the girls to bed on time, with just five small bathrooms to share between them. However, as with mealtimes, they'd been programmed to operate at high speed. When I went to check the youngest girls were in bed at 9.30 p.m., I was pleasantly surprised to find them all snuggled up in bed in their pyjamas, cuddling teddies, and with reading books in hand. None of the books were the ones I had set them to read in class, and I didn't know whether to be pleased about that or not.

It was fascinating to see how each girl marked her territory around her bed with a halo of posters, magazine cuttings, and photographs on the wall behind it. There were family snaps, solo selfies, group shots of girls on school outings. Among them I spotted a few famous faces: royals, film stars, or high-flying business types, but I did not enquire about the girls' relationships to them, knowing Miss Harnett preferred equal status for all. Of course, I kept a surreptitious lookout for the colour plates that might have come from the bursar's vandalised library book, but found none.

I was startled to discover beside one girl's bed a large cardboard cut-out that at first I mistook for a real man. He was dressed in evening wear and held a gun in his hand, looking like the poster for a James Bond film.

Imogen must have heard me gasp.

'Don't mind Daddy,' she said cheerily, putting her arms round his two-dimensional self for a hug and a kiss before climbing into her bed. 'The gun's not real.'

'What are you going to read us tonight, miss?' asked Tilly from the bed in the far corner, busy plaiting her long dark hair, presumably to keep it tangle-free overnight.

That took me by surprise. 'Me? Now? Read to you?'

'Miss Bliss always reads to us for fifteen minutes.'

I wondered why Oriana hadn't included that in my briefing. Were they having me on?

'Really? What does she read?'

'*The Adventures of Pippi Longstocking,*' they chorused, clearly relishing the name.

'Aren't you...?' I began, and was about to say 'too old for these stories', which I remembered enjoying back in primary school. But as I clocked their eager, hopeful faces, soft in the low light cast from their bedside lamps, I realised the connection: they shared the motherless Pippi's vulnerability. Seeing her sea-captain father only at rare intervals, she claimed complete self-reliance and gloried in her independence, though her more conventional friends suspected her of making up her madcap adventures to hide her loneliness.

'Pippi Longstocking it is, then,' I beamed, gratefully accepting the big green hardback that Imogen held out to me.

I looked around the room. 'Where does Miss Bliss usually sit to read to you?' There were no armchairs, just a low hard stool beside each bed, all now draped with discarded school uniform. Tilly pointed to the empty bed opposite Imogen's. The bursar had mentioned there were still a few vacancies for pupils, and I remembered now that in each dorm there'd been at least one empty bed and dressing table. Each House could have accommodated thirty girls, not the twenty-five I had in mine. What a difference those extra school fees would make to balancing the bursar's budget.

I slipped my shoes off on to the faded bedside rug and climbed on to the wooden bed, at the foot of which lay a blanket made of knitted squares, presumably the product of a house project. Settling down on to the sagging mattress, I pulled the blanket over my legs, feeling the chill as the central heating in the dorms went off after bedtime. I opened the book at the bookmark and took a deep breath. One chapter should be plenty, I thought, glancing up at the girls' eager faces.

As I read, the girls gradually clicked off their bedside lights, until I was conscious of sitting in a dark room, the only lamp still illuminated focused on *Pippi*. Halfway through the second chapter, I glanced around to check how many of the girls were asleep and realised that while I had been reading they had all styled their hair into two plaits, which they'd arranged at right angles to their heads, draped across their pillows. Each had closed her eyes, slight chests gently rising and falling in the comfortable rhythm of sleep. Perhaps they were all Pippi Longstocking in their dreams, reliving the chapter in which her father returned home from the sea.

For a moment I closed my eyes too, leaning back against the headboard, wondering what my own parents were doing right now. What had I been thinking to neglect them for so long, simply to keep Steven sweet, prioritising his needs over theirs? These girls here were separated from their families by their fathers' volition, their boarding the by-product of demanding jobs and deceased mothers, not through any fault of their own. I had no such excuse.

22

THE YELLOW WALLPAPER

I stirred as I felt something touch my cheek. Feather-light but unexpected, it was enough to wake me. As I sat upright, the Pippi Longstocking book slipped from my hands on to the mattress as McPhee made himself comfortable on my lap.

Miss Harnett, standing by my bed, smiled at me and spoke in a low voice so as not to wake the children. 'My dear, you must have nodded off. Are Pippi's adventures not sufficiently exciting for you?'

I blinked and rubbed my eyes. 'To be honest, I rather enjoyed them. What time is it, please?'

'Just gone ten thirty. The younger girls are all asleep, and I've made sure the older girls have turned their lights out. I suggest you toddle back to your flat for an early night. You look as if you could do with one.'

'Is Oriana back yet?'

My heart began to beat a little faster as I remembered her date with Steven. I hoped she was safe. Surely on her first date he would be on his best behaviour, to win her over. There should still be time for me to warn her off him, before she could come to any serious harm.

'I've no idea, but if the girls need you, they'll knock on your door. They know where you are. Just don't leave your flat till after midnight in case they come calling.'

I smiled. 'Don't worry, I don't plan to leave it till breakfast time.' I slid my legs round to place my feet on the floor and into my shoes and returned the book to the bedside table. 'Did you need me, by the way? Is that why you came to find me?'

Scooping up McPhee and draping the cat over her shoulder like a fur stole, she took my arm companionably and led me to the door. Out in the corridor we were able to speak above a whisper without disturbing the girls.

'My dear, I always end each day with a little stroll among my sleeping beauties, to make sure they're all settled. When it's quiet at night and the rest of the dorm is sleeping around you, it's easy for some little soul to feel overwhelmed by loneliness and homesickness, especially those furthest from home. I aim to nip such feelings in the bud and provide an antidote.'

She tickled McPhee behind the ears, and I reached out to stroke him myself, smiling at his half-closed amber eyes. A cat with such an affectionate temperament should enjoy the post of Comforter to Homesick Girls.

'What about you?' I asked her as we were about to part company at the top of the stairs. 'Are you all done for the night? Do you ever have an evening off? It strikes me that you're always on duty.'

Looking weary for a moment, she gazed down the marble staircase. 'Once a headmistress...' she began. Then she brightened. 'But there are compensations. I do have the best dorm.'

Her eyes twinkled. Oriana had told me Miss Harnett's bedroom had once been Lord Bunting's. Apparently it was fabulous. And I bet the bursar was dead jealous, tucked away like a servant in the gatehouse.

She gave a little wave of her free hand and began to glide gracefully down the stairs. 'Sleep well, my dear,' she called over her shoulder.

I watched as she turned at the foot of the stairs, wondering whether her bed was the same one Lord Bunting had slept in, and whether McPhee was allowed on it with her. Then I headed for my own flat. It might not have been as lavish as hers, but I was thankful to have it. I was more determined than ever to make a success of this job, to earn the right to stay here.

Before I reached my own front door, I passed Oriana's and saw it was ajar. I wondered how she'd got on with Steven on their date, if indeed that's what it was. I tapped lightly on her door and called her name.

No reply. I knocked harder, as we were far enough from the dorms not to wake the girls. I wouldn't be able to sleep until I knew she had come home safely.

'Oriana, it's me, Gemma. Fancy a cup of cocoa with me?' I was getting rather addicted to school cocoa.

Hearing no reply, I assumed she was still out and had left her door unlocked by mistake. I wondered whether one of the girls had come to find her and was waiting inside, lonely and distressed. I didn't like to intrude into Oriana's private space, but duty called. Remaining on the threshold, I gently pushed the door, letting it swing open slowly so as not to startle whichever girl was within.

'Hello, it's only me. It's Miss Lamb. Miss Bliss is still out. Can I help you?'

When I reached inside the door to flick on the light, my mouth fell open with surprise. The walls of Oriana's flat were completely covered in yellow banknotes. Floor to ceiling, wall to wall, every inch of the room was plastered with money.

I stepped in to touch it, to check whether it was really only novelty wallpaper, but the edges of each note were palpable. They were real currency. In a few places notes were coming away from the wall at the corners.

How rich must Oriana be to paper her walls with banknotes? And how selfish and frivolous to fritter it away like this when the school was in such financial need? Could all of this money really be the fruits of her pursuit of rich widowed fathers? Maybe she didn't need me to warn her of Steven at all – as soon as she realised he didn't have that kind of money, she'd move on of her own accord.

I read the lettering on one of the notes. This benefactor must have been Bolivian, as the currency was called the Bolivar, which was new to me.

I had a flashback to the expensive wallpaper with which Steven had insisted on creating a supposedly fashionable feature wall in his lounge. It was hand-printed paper at £485 a roll. What would he give to have a flat decorated with such an ostentatious show of wealth? And if Oriana's walls were covered in money, what other valuables might have been tucked away under her bed or left lying around with no thought for security?

Then I remembered why I'd come in.

'Hello, anybody there?' I called again, louder this time.

This room was certainly empty, and the kitchenette and bathroom lay in darkness. I flicked on their light switches, to assure myself that these rooms were also unoccupied. Had Oriana inadvertently left the door unlocked when she went out, or had someone broken in? A potential intruder getting past Max's vigilance? Surely not. But just in case, I thought I'd better alert him, especially with all this money lying about.

Leaving Oriana's front door ajar, I retreated next door to my own flat, lifted the handset for my landline, and pressed the school's speed-dial number for Max.

23

ORIANA INVADED

'Security.' Max answered the call almost before it had rung.

'Hi, Max, it's Gemma.'

'I know.' Of course he did.

'I'm worried about Oriana. She's gone out for her evening off and she's not back yet, but her flat door was wide open. She's normally meticulous about keeping it locked to protect her privacy. I've never even been in there before. I'm worried someone might have broken in to steal something. All that money, for a start.'

'Money?'

'On her walls.'

'Ha!'

'Yes, really. Have you not seen it? It's there for the taking.'

Max sighed. 'Listen, Gemma, to put your mind at rest, I'll come up and have a look. But don't worry, there won't be any thieves on the prowl, nor any other kind of intruder. You can sleep easy in your bed tonight. I expect in her haste to get away for her night off, Oriana didn't lock her door properly. It's a windy night and these corridors can be draughty. A gust of wind could have been enough to push it open if it wasn't locked.'

I wondered where Max was, hoping he wouldn't take long to arrive.

'But what about all that cash? Isn't it just putting temptation in people's way? For the girls, as well as for intruders? Or even staff.' I hoped Mavis hadn't got wind of it. 'There must be a fortune stuck to her walls.'

'In her dreams,' he murmured, hanging up.

I wished I was wealthy enough to dismiss a big stash of cash so lightly. Was Max rich too? I got up to put the kettle on to make us both some cocoa, feeling guilty for calling Max out on such a wet and windy night if this was to prove a wild goose chase.

With his usual lightning reactions, Max was outside my flat before the kettle had even boiled. But no sooner had I made us both a mug of cocoa than Oriana was knocking at my front door. She must have just returned from her date. I'd forgotten she said she'd check with me when she got back that my dorm duty had gone smoothly.

'Oh, Oriana, hello,' I began. 'I'm so glad to see you. I called Max because the door to your flat was wide open and I was worried there might have been a break-in.'

Her smile faded. 'To my flat? I don't think so. Any thief in his right mind would target the bursary, where all the big money is kept. Besides, no intruder's ever got past Max before.'

Max raised his mug in a toast to her compliment.

Even though she was making me feel foolish and very

much still the new girl, I was so relieved that she was okay that I didn't mind.

'My flat is my private domain,' she continued, folding her arms across her chest in defiance. 'And I'll thank you to stay out of it in future.'

With that she turned on her heel and stalked back to her front door, slamming it behind her. Max and I stood in silence as the sound echoed down the corridor.

For a moment, I wondered whether her rage was connected with Caroline's transgression. Caroline had let someone else into her flat – a governor – and something unspeakable had resulted. Was this why Oriana found my act of trespass so heinous?

Max winked at me. 'I'm guessing someone's date didn't go well.'

Whatever the cause of Oriana's bad mood, this did not seem the right moment to warn her any further about Steven.

'Thanks for coming over, Max, and sorry to have brought you out for nothing on such a horrible night.'

'It's no problem, Gemma; it's what they pay me for. And I'm glad if I'm able to reassure you.'

I smiled at him. 'Yes. Yes, you do.'

24

UNDERVALUED

I did no more than pick at my breakfast the next day, setting a bad example to the girls. I was hoping to catch Oriana straight after breakfast on the pretext of apologising for invading her private space, but really to warn her further about Steven. However, she dismissed her table and slipped out of the dining hall long before I could escape to speak to her. My girls all seemed ravenous this morning, offering each other extras of everything, and were still chomping when the bell went.

I also failed to catch Oriana when we walked across to the classroom quad for the first lesson, glimpsing her only as she closed her classroom door behind her. She didn't appear in the staffroom for morning coffee, either.

Nicolette touched my arm as I queued for my turn at Old Faithful.

'Ah, *ma belle*, you do not look happy,' she said gently. '*Qu'est-ce que c'est?*'

I didn't mean to be so transparent, nor did I want to involve anyone else in my tale of embarrassment. But when Nicolette fixed her kind eyes on mine, I couldn't help but want to confide in her. I looked back imploringly.

'Bring your coffee over to my corner where no one will hear us,' she said in a low voice, watching me pour in the milk.

Nicolette normally shared a battered old two-seater sofa with her handbag, occasionally inviting another teacher to join her there for a confidential chat. Present at St Bride's simply because she needed a live-in post while teaching in a foreign country, rather than because she was running away from something, she was in the best position to counsel the rest of us on our woes. As a result, she was the staffroom's unofficial agony aunt.

She waited patiently while I stirred my steaming coffee to cool it down.

'Nicolette, I'm worried that I upset Oriana last night. I did something foolish.'

'Last night? Her night off? *Ah oui!* You cover for her in the Poorhouse. What happened? I hope the girls did not themselves misbehave?'

I took another sip. 'Oh no, the girls were as good as gold. In fact, I enjoyed spending the evening with them, getting to know them better.' I hadn't realised this until I said it, but it was true.

She waited for me to continue in my own time, sipping her black coffee elegantly.

'But after lights out, when I went back to my flat, I saw Oriana's door was open and I thought perhaps a girl had come to find her in her absence and might need my help. So I went in to look, but the sitting room was empty, and Oriana was still out. Then I was scared there might be intruders, what with the door being left open, so I sent for Max. When Oriana got back, she was livid to find I'd been in her flat.'

'Perhaps she did not have a good evening with your boyfriend?'

So Oriana's date with Steven was common knowledge.

'Ex-boyfriend. How did you know about that?'

Nicolette bit back a smile. 'When I look at how she dresses just now, and her lighter, prettier hair...' She cast her eyes over me from head to toe. 'I do not need to be the genius. So did she have a good evening? Do you know?'

She touched my hand where it gripped the handle of my now empty cup.

'I— I don't know. I haven't had a chance to ask.'

For a moment I wondered whether it would be wise to confide in Nicolette about my fears concerning Steven, then I decided it would be best to keep them to a need-to-know basis. I didn't want the whole school to know how weak and foolish I had been to let myself be treated so badly by him. What sort of role model would I be for young girls if my past was public knowledge?

'To be honest,' I continued, 'my main concern at that point was that her flat had been burgled, as the door was open and I saw that foreign currency all over her walls.' I moved closer to Nicolette and lowered my voice. 'Did you know about all her money? Talk about putting temptation in people's way!'

Nicolette sat back and laughed, not unkindly. '*Ma belle*, do not imagine a burglar would break in with a machine of steam to remove Oriana's money from her walls. It is not worth it.'

'Why not?' Was Nicolette another from Joe's Trust Fund Brigade too comfortably off to be covetous of others' wealth?

'But there are hundreds of banknotes on her walls. If she's that ostentatious with her money, how much more might she have tucked away out of sight? And if she hasn't got anything better to do with it than paper the walls, why not donate it to the school, for everyone's benefit?'

Nicolette smiled. '*Ma chérie*, did you notice the currency? Were they your pounds of sterling? *Non*. My own Euros? *Mais non*.'

'No, they were something in Spanish or possibly Portuguese. As Spain and Portugal are in the Eurozone, I assumed they must be South American. Bolivian, I think. Yes, they were Bolivars.'

Nicolette smiled. 'Venezuelan. The Bolivars of Venezuela. A souvenir of the very big inflation. Like the Reichsmark in Germany before the war. In those days, you needed a wheelbarrow full of money to buy a loaf of bread.'

I considered for a moment. 'I wonder how much money it would have taken to pay for a wheelbarrow.'

Nicolette laughed. 'Oriana is playing a joke. She is trying hard to laugh at herself, and at Señor Escobar, the Venezuelan gentleman who broke her heart. When his daughter was at St Bride's, he took a fancy to Oriana, but he let her down badly.'

Uninvited, Joe came to perch beside me on the arm of Nicolette's sofa. 'Oriana's also putting two fingers up to the bursar for changing her savings into Bolivars in the first place. Honestly, Oriana can twist the bursar round her little finger, but for her own good he ought to have stood up to her and refused. He must have known the Bolivars would soon be worthless. Sometimes I wonder whether he is in the right job.'

'Worthless? Really?' I gasped. Poor Oriana.

'Just like the Reichsmark,' said Nicolette, nodding. 'That's why Escobar hadn't paid his daughter's fees. In Bolivars, Escobar was a billionaire – but the Bolivars were worth no more than toilet paper.'

'In Venezuela, sheet for sheet, toilet paper was probably worth more.' Joe grinned at his own joke. 'Poor old Miss Bliss didn't realise. She believed what she wanted to believe, until too late. Wretched buzzard did a bunk, taking his daughter with him, leaving her school fees unpaid and just an apologetic farewell note for Oriana, saying he was going on the run to avoid his creditors. God knows where he and his poor daughter are now.'

I gasped again. 'Poor Oriana! What kind of heel dumps his girlfriend with a note and goes into hiding?'

Joe bit back a smile, but chivalrously did not mention my treatment of Steven.

'And poor bursar,' said Nicolette. 'She was very cold to him for months. It made him very sad.'

'And Oriana was broken-hearted for at least a week,' said Joe, a mischievous glint in his eyes.

'But Oriana, she is strong,' said Nicolette. 'She is hard to break.'

'Like a self-healing phone screen,' said Joe cheerily. 'Easily dropped and cracked, but rights itself in no time at all. At least your Steven operates in pounds sterling.'

'Joscelyn, you are a teaspoon,' said Nicolette, lightly slapping Joe's bare thigh.

'You mean a stirrer,' he replied.

'But I do not think Oriana behaves well. She should not be

unkind to Gemma, and she should not take her boyfriend. Oriana herself embarrasses.'

I was touched by Nicolette's consideration, but it was Oriana who deserved more concern.

'Don't worry, Nicolette, I'll be fine. And to be honest, Steven's no catch to say the least. We're both far better off without him. And thank you for telling me about Mr Escobar. I understand Oriana better now.'

Taking Nicolette's cup and saucer from her hand, I returned it with mine to the trolley, gathered up my papers for the next lesson, and left the staffroom feeling far better than when I'd come in.

* * *

As I sat marking essays at my classroom desk, I began to feel a little calmer. I tried to tell myself that perhaps things would work out for Oriana and Steven after all. A young British businessman on the upward trajectory of his career might be glad of an elegant and accomplished girlfriend, or even a wife. Far healthier for her to latch on to an unattached, independent, childless man of around her own age than the widowed fathers of teenagers, incapable of providing enough care at home to educate their daughters locally. Besides, who knew what baggage they had? The only baggage Steven had, according to him anyway, was me. Yes, Oriana would be much better for him than I could ever be, provided she could control his temper and rid him of his possessive jealousy... I shook myself. What on earth was I thinking? As if any woman should have to control a man's temper... I was going around in circles.

I felt something warm brush against my ankles, a comforting touch. I leaned into it and lowered my hand to stroke my furry visitor.

'Hello, McPhee.' I tickled him, or her, behind the ears. 'You're quite right, I shouldn't be thinking of myself as Steven's baggage, even if he did call me that – and worse – enough times.'

McPhee nudged me again, wanting me to continue to stroke him. But my thoughts were far away.

Whatever else had happened between Oriana and Steven the previous night, had she let him know that I was here? While she might have managed some dissembling when turning him away on his first visit, it was hard to believe that they could have spent an evening together with no reference to me. Though it was conceivable that she might not have mentioned me to avoid distracting him from herself.

But it really was none of my business, was it? Shouldn't I do the decent thing and tactically withdraw, leaving them the best possible chance to build a new relationship together? My priorities now should be to concentrate on making a go of this job, thereby keeping my staff flat, even if it meant finding a way to resolve the school's financial crisis. Even so, I told myself I would warn Oriana the first chance I got, and then let her decide what she wanted for herself.

25

THE WISDOM OF THE POORHOUSE

'She's had another one, you know,' said Imogen darkly to her neighbour at lunchtime. I followed her gaze across to the table that Oriana was supervising. For a moment I thought she was referring to her housemistress's latest man. When her friend replied, I was glad I hadn't admonished her.

'From Harrods again too,' said Poppy, rolling her eyes. 'In a box so big you could sit in it.'

'I would be happy if my dad just sent me the box,' piped up Tilly. 'With some cushions and a blanket, it would make a cosy den.'

Sometimes I forgot just how young the youngest pupils were.

'The thing is, not even the full box makes Veronica happy, although she pretends it does,' said Imogen. 'She doesn't even like half the contents. Honestly, you'd think her dad would know that she doesn't like pink things or white chocolate. She's not a baby.'

'No, but I do,' said Tilly with a grin. 'She gave me a whole bunch of white chocolate roses to thank me for helping her with her French prep last night.'

There was a silence for a moment while the girls chewed thoughtfully on their sandwiches.

'I expect his secretary ordered it,' said Imogen, passing me the pastries basket. 'That's what they have secretaries for.'

When I declined and took it to offer to her, she helped herself to a sausage roll.

'If I was her, I'd have saved all the things in it to give as birthday or Christmas presents to my friends,' said Poppy.

'She'd need more friends than there are girls in the school to get through that many presents,' said Imogen.

I gazed across at Oriana's table. 'Which girl is it we're talking about?'

'The one on Miss Blister's right,' said Imogen.

I recognised Veronica as a quiet girl who seldom contributed in class. I'd wondered whether she was one of the heiresses, as her large stud earrings, the only real jewellery the girls were allowed to wear, looked like real diamonds, and on her wrist was a top-of-the-range smartwatch.

'Last exeat she invited me to stay at her London house,' said Poppy. 'It was amazing. We spent most of the weekend in her underground swimming pool playing spies.'

'What was her dad like?' asked Imogen.

Poppy shrugged. 'I don't know. I never saw him. Her nanny was nice though. She taught us to swear in Bulgarian.'

'If I did her maths prep for her, do you think she'd let me have the empty box?' asked Tilly.

'You could post yourself home in it,' said Poppy.

'I think Veronica would rather her father posted himself in

it than all that stuff.' Imogen licked a fingertip to pick up a
stray sunflower seed from her plate. 'Please may we leave the
table, miss?'

'Yes, girls, thank you.' I remained in my seat while they all
scraped back their chairs and departed, then got up to go just
as Oriana dismissed her table. Veronica, lingering after the
others had gone, was solemnly presenting Oriana with a
chunky pink ballpoint pen containing twelve different
coloured inks. When Oriana thanked her profusely for her
kindness, Veronica gave a flicker of a smile before running off
to catch up with her friends.

Oriana held up the pen to show me as she got to her feet.

'Unwanted gift,' she said. 'We're not really meant to accept
gifts from the girls except for at Christmas, birthdays, and the
end of the academic year, but it would be churlish to refuse
Veronica. I wonder if her father realises the chief pleasure she
gets from his constant lavish gift boxes is giving the contents
away?'

I was relieved to find that Oriana seemed to have forgiven
my intrusion into her flat, and we strolled across the hall
together, keeping our voices low so the girls wouldn't overhear.

'I suppose it must make her popular,' I said.

Oriana wrinkled her nose. 'Not really. The other girls just
feel sorry for her.'

I made a mental note to be especially attentive to Veronica
in class.

'I can understand that. I bet she'd rather swap the whole
box for a personal letter or email from her dad.'

Oriana leapt to his defence. 'Poor man is far too busy. He's
very high up at the London Stock Exchange, you know.'

I wondered whether Oriana had ever targeted Veronica's dad.

'Anyway, speaking of men...,' she began and opened the staffroom door for me, standing back to let me go through first, '...are you sure about me seeing Steven? You really don't mind?'

I took that as an instruction as much as a question: it seemed she was really telling me not to mind. I decided it was time to speak up.

'It's not that I mind, exactly, Oriana. I mean, you're welcome to him. But to be honest, I think you haven't seen the real Steven yet, and there's something I need to warn you about. You see, he's very controlling once he gets to know you and has a terrible temper.'

'Ha! I've yet to meet a man who could control me!' She tossed her head. 'Honestly, I appreciate your concern, but there's really no need. I'm my own person, Gemma. I call the shots in my relationships. I'm no Caroline.' She stopped short, her hand to her mouth. 'Anyway, the thing is,' she went on, 'I'm seeing him again at the weekend. He's invited me to Sunday lunch. And Saturday supper, in fact.'

I didn't want to think about what might happen in between. But I was glad I'd warned her, and even gladder to realise that I wouldn't have swapped places with her for the world.

26

COOLING DOWN

Halfway through Poppy's surprisingly mature reading of 'Daffodils' – we'd just started the Romantics, as per the Year Seven curriculum pinned up inside my store cupboard – I shivered.

When we'd started working our way through the battered red hardbacks of 'Great British Poetry', I remembered I'd loved these poems myself at their age and wondered why I'd barely picked up a poetry book lately, since there was so much pleasure to be found in them. But Steven didn't like me reading poetry, or anything else, really, seeing books as rivals for attention. I'd stopped reading anything humorous too, as it annoyed him if I laughed at what he perceived as private jokes that excluded him. Whenever I'd tried to share them by reading aloud to him, he'd remained stony-faced.

'What's the point of reading P. G. Wodehouse now?' he'd said once, annoyed at the tears of laughter rolling down my face. 'The man's been dead for years.'

As for romantic novels – I'd stopped reading those long

ago. They just depressed me, demonstrating what was missing from my life.

But why should 'Daffodils' make me shiver now? I raised my eyes from my copy of the book in which I was following Poppy's rendition. Every girl in the room had not only buttoned her cardigan to her neck, she'd also pulled a pashmina from her book bag and wrapped it round her shoulders. The scattering of so many coloured wraps reminded me of a tin of Quality Street.

Imogen caught me staring at her purple shawl and pulled it tighter about her shoulders, wrapping her hands in the loose ends.

'Didn't you bring yours with you, miss? My sister told us we'll need them as the term goes by.'

Imogen's big sister was three years ahead of her.

'Don't worry, I'll just turn the radiator up.'

I jumped down from my seat and strolled over to put my hand on the huge white-painted edifice under the window. It was stone cold. I drew back my hand.

'Dear me, it's not on at all.'

I tried turning the little metal wheel that connected the radiator to the pipes, thinking the valve might not have been open.

'My sister says the bursar won't put the heating on in the daytime until after half-term,' said Imogen.

That would be the start of November. How desperate must the school's finances be to deprive the girls of any heating at this time of year?

'I'm sure that can't be right. Now, who would like to read "Kubla Khan"?'

I thought its exotic setting might fool us into feeling warmer.

At the end of the lesson, as the girls were packing their books away, I checked the radiator again, only to find it as cold as a dead poet.

'No luck, miss?' Poppy stopped on her way to the door to give me a second opinion, then snatched her chilled hand away from the icy metal to warm it in her cardigan pocket.

I shook my head. 'Perhaps there's a blockage. I'll report it to the bursar after lunch so he can fix it.'

Imogen rolled her eyes at me. 'Good luck with that, miss. He says he doesn't feel the cold at all.'

'He says, "If I don't feel the cold at my age, nor should you".' Poppy's impression of the bursar's gruff tones was even more impressive than her reading of 'Daffodils'.

'That's why we all have thermals, miss,' said Imogen. 'To keep us alive until November.'

'If we don't go home at half-term to warm up, we'll probably all die of hypochondria,' added Poppy.

'You mean hypothermia, Poppy. But it's not that cold. Besides, you've all got your lovely pashminas.'

As I followed them into the quad, there was no appreciable difference between the temperature inside and out. If anything, the quad was warmer as the sun had come out and the flagstones were soaking up its heat. As I dawdled across the courtyard, warming up as I went, I googled 'legal minimum temperature in schools' and downloaded a useful briefing note from the National Union of Teachers to get the facts.

As I entered the bursar's office in response to his imperious 'Come!', the heat inside hit me like a wall.

'Nice and cosy in here,' I remarked. 'So the school heating must be working then?' I glanced at the log fire blazing in the grate. 'I wish I had one of these in my classroom. My radiator's stone cold, you know.'

The bursar set down his fountain pen and sat back, dwarfed as usual by his swivel chair.

'You exaggerate, Gemma. Perhaps having come to us from a city centre, you're not used to the seasons. Country people don't aspire to live at the same temperature all year round, you know. I expect you'll be clamouring for air conditioning in the summer term.'

He put his hands behind his head and regarded me steadily.

'Gemma, do you have any idea how much it costs to heat this place for a single day? If you had to pay the bills, as I do, you wouldn't be so quick to complain.'

I frowned.

'I'm not concerned for myself. I have my girls to think of. I can't expect them to learn well if they're chilled through.'

'That's why we ask them to bring pashminas and thermals. We tell them they're being environmentally friendly.'

He propelled his chair over to a set of filing trays beneath the window and extracted a copy of the school uniform list. Wheeling himself back behind his desk, he pushed the list across to me.

'There. You see? The girls need to show a sense of responsibility for their own well-being.'

He returned his attention to the pad he'd been writing on when I came in, as if considering the case closed.

The thought of those poor little girls shivering in their luxury wraps made me bold. I pulled out my phone and tapped the screen to retrieve the download from the NUT, highlighting the passage on responsibilities.

'See, you have to provide a thermometer to give evidence that you're heating the classrooms to the legal minimum. There's no thermometer in my classroom. Please provide one.'

He took the phone from my hand and peered at the downloaded document through the lower half of his bifocals. 'A sufficient number of thermometers should be available... blah blah blah... they do not, however, require a thermometer to be provided in every room.'

I scanned his office and my eyes alighted on an antique wooden thermometer on his wall. I crossed the room to read it. 'It's twenty-five degrees in here. Can I borrow this for the afternoon, please? I'll bring it back after last lesson.'

He held up a hand to stay me. 'No, wait, I've got a much more portable one.' He rummaged in his desk drawer and produced a digital device that I recognised as being from IKEA. 'Turn it this way up and it tells you the temperature. This way shows you the time. Turn it again for the stopwatch and this way if you want the date.'

He set it down on the date side and gazed at me in defiance.

I picked it up and turned it to read the temperature: twenty-five degrees again. It was accurate, at least.

As he slid the drawer closed, I picked up the thermometer and headed for the door. As I passed the fireplace, I considered prolonging the conversation so that I could linger in its warmth, but decided his chilly personality would cancel out any heat gain.

As I left his office, he was slipping off his suit jacket and hanging it over the back of his chair.

27

FLAT CHECK

I arrived in the library to find Mavis sitting at her usual desk wearing a thick fur coat. On hearing my footsteps, she looked up and uttered a dismissive 'Ha!' at the sight of the green plastic cube in my hand.

'Let me guess: that thing's telling you it's twenty-five degrees in here?'

When I turned the device to show her its reading, she rolled her eyes.

'Up to his old tricks as soon as the mercury drops,' she said. 'I've never seen that thermometer read anything other than twenty-five degrees. I don't know who the bursar thinks he's fooling. If I was in the National Union of Teachers, I'd have my rep down on him like a ton of bricks. I can't imagine why Hairnet allows it when she's so solicitous of the girls' well-being in every other respect.'

'Needs must, I suppose. It must cost a fortune to heat this place. I don't suppose it's ever been properly insulated like a modern building.'

I gazed up at the high ceiling and the vast picture windows that ran two sides of the room.

Mavis nodded. 'You get used to it after a while, I promise you.' She fastened the buttons on her coat. 'Not least because you get into the habit of wearing more. Look at this.'

She held out an arm to demonstrate the thickness of the fur and beckoned me to stroke it. My fingers sank deep into the silky pile.

'Goodness, you must be snug in that.'

'If it was good enough for a bear on the Russian steppes, it's good enough for a St Bride's schoolteacher.'

I shrank back. 'Bear? Really? Goodness! Is that even legal in this country?'

Mavis shrugged. 'Who knows? I didn't buy it. I could never afford a fur coat, not even second-hand. No, it was a gift from a grateful Russian parent. He personally imported one for each of us who taught his little Olga for the year she spent here.'

'He must have had trouble getting that lot into his baggage allowance.'

'Not really. He came in his own private jet.'

I wondered how his arrival on the scene had influenced Oriana's dress sense that year.

'I don't generally wear it around school unless it's really cold, as the sight of it upsets the girls.'

'Why, do they miss Olga?'

'No, they never took to Olga. But they do worry about what happened to the rest of the bear.'

'What about the rest of Olga? Did she change schools because she was unhappy here?'

'No, she had to flee Europe after her father's arrest. She

now lives in style in some small Central American republic, on a passport from a tiny Caribbean island nation that she'd had up her sleeve all along just in case something like that happened. A lot of them do. The headmistress had a tip-off in sufficient time for Max to whisk Olga to the airport and put her on a flight to Panama.'

'The poor girl. How frightening. I'd have been terrified in her shoes.'

'Oh no, she was more than equal to the challenge. She'd been raised to expect such disruptions. And more than happy to move to a Caribbean climate, after a year at St Bride's.'

I looked longingly at the coat, determining to buy some thermal underwear over the internet as soon as I had a moment to myself.

'Doesn't Miss Hairnet feel the cold? She's quite an old lady, so you'd think she would.'

When Mavis flinched, I realised she might have been older than the head.

'Not her. She's the most used to the cold out of all of us. She's been here forever.'

'You mean she's only ever taught here?'

Mavis nodded. 'She even went to school here. And in those days, they didn't have hot running water in the bathrooms in the dormitories. It came out of the taps freezing cold, or not at all, if the temperature outside was sub-zero. They had to break the ice in the water jugs for their basins.'

I shuddered.

'Wow. Mind you, she has got beautiful skin. There's barely a line on it. Maybe that's why.'

'At least our flats are cosy,' Mavis added gratefully. 'The

accommodation areas – the dorms and staff flats – are in the oldest part of the building with the thickest walls and working fireplaces.'

I nodded, looking forward to a blazing log fire in my flat after supper. Not even the bursar could grumble about that, as the logs didn't cost him a penny – they came from trees coppiced on the school estate. I wondered what the temperature would be in my flat now. I decided to check as a before and after exercise.

* * *

In the Poorhouse corridor, I bumped into Oriana, who laughed when she saw the thermometer in my hand.

'Honestly, how stupid does the bursar think we are?' she scoffed. 'Not as stupid as he is, luckily for us. I don't know why I ever trust him with anything.'

'I was just going to leave it in my flat to see whether it changes while we're having supper.'

'You can put it in your fridge and it'll still say twenty-five degrees. I don't know who he thinks he is fooling.'

She waited for me to unlock my door, slip the thermometer inside, and return to accompany her down to the Trough.

'So, what are your plans for exeat weekend?' Oriana asked.

'Exeat?'

'This term's first exeat is this weekend. You're off the hook from Saturday morning till Sunday teatime. Will you go away for the weekend?'

I shook my head quickly. 'I have no plans. Just to stay here and catch up with a bit of reading, perhaps.'

The thought of having the library to myself, and the splendid gardens, seemed a real treat.

We walked on in silence for a moment, and I realised she was waiting for me to ask about her plans for the weekend. Perhaps she'd forgotten I already knew them.

I played it safe by asking a simple question. 'So you're spending the whole weekend with Steven?'

She beamed at the prospect.

'Yes, and I can't begin to tell you how refreshing it is to have met someone I don't have to see only at the start and finish of terms when they're delivering or collecting their daughter.'

Poor Oriana. No matter how busy or important these men were, there was no excuse to treat her like that.

'He's going to pick me up in that gorgeous car of his on Saturday after breakfast and bring me back in time for Sunday tea.' She giggled. 'I'll feel just like one of the girls.'

That made me feel a bit uncomfortable, but I was genuinely glad she was happy for a change, despite my reservations about Steven. Maybe he'd be different with her – I hoped he'd be different with her.

'Is he taking you anywhere nice?'

'Just to his apartment,' she said lightly, as we crossed the hall to the Trough. 'I'm looking forward to seeing his place.'

I kept my face expressionless. 'It's a bit different from here.'

She smiled again. 'That's no bad thing. Sometimes you can have too much of all this old stuff.'

I thought back to Steven's low ceilings, plain modern windows, and IKEA furniture. Hardly the grand environment that Oriana was used to. Still, at least he could afford to pay his fuel bills and he kept the thermostat turned up.

I swung open the Trough door and stood back to let her in.

Don't give him my love, I wanted to say. Then I realised he'd never really had it anyway.

28

SILENT SATURDAY

The school felt a little eerie without the pupils. As I strolled down the corridor around midday on Saturday, my footsteps echoed in the stillness like they had when I'd come to my job interview back in the summer. That day I'd been daunted first by the grandeur of the building, then by the bursar's coolness as he'd showed me to Miss Harnett's study. I'd only begun to relax once I was in her kindly company.

Now I felt a sense of ownership, not only of my flat, where I'd marked my territory by rearranging the furniture and adding a few personal touches, such as my favourite books and photos of my parents, but of the whole building. My pride in its grand architecture grew as it became more familiar. I often wondered which person in its past had left the scuffmarks of prior residence behind them: the dent in a brass doorknob, the chip in a carved wooden cornice, the missing threads from an antique rug. Perhaps I'd make a permanent mark of my own before I left. The place oozed history and heritage, and in a very small way I felt as if I was becoming a thread in its vast tapestry.

After breakfast that Saturday morning, the girls had been bundled out of the great double doors at the front of the building to a car park full of top-of-the-range cars, driven by doting fathers, nannies, or chauffeurs. A minibus had hoovered up the rest of the girls to take them to the nearest railway station to catch the next London train.

The minute the last vehicle had gone, a bevy of teachers had swept out of the doors to claim their own cars and speed off down the drive before the dust had even settled. Most had other accommodation outside of term time, places they owned or family homes to return to, or else they stayed with friends. The staff slept in school only during term time, and I'd received pitying looks in the staffroom when I'd confessed I'd be spending the weekend on site.

'It'll be handy to have some free time to decorate my class-room properly,' I'd told them with forced heartiness. 'I've heaps of ideas for extending the girls' learning now that I've settled in, and I want to put up some new displays to stimulate them.'

To my surprise, I'd realised this was true. I was settling in as a teacher, finding my stride, building a good rapport with the girls, and feeling increasingly confident.

I was also taking pleasure from proving Steven wrong. For so long, I'd let him deter me from taking up the profession that I'd planned to join since I was not much older than St Bride's youngest. He'd claimed at first he'd been charmed by my quiet nature but he'd soon turned it against me, saying he couldn't imagine me keeping order in a classroom. I'd tried not to let him convince me, but when I'd found the perfect job for a newly qualified teacher in the local private boys' school, he'd kept on at me with so many objections that I'd let the deadline pass without applying. Only when it had been too late had he let slip the real reason: I'd have been the only female member of staff in the English department. He hadn't wanted me meeting other single men who might have led me astray. Well, astray from him, anyway.

No matter. I was here now and pursuing my original ambition. I was even turning out to be good at it. In my next job, perhaps in a state school, I'd earn enough to rent or buy my own flat. I might even get a decent reference from Hairnet, for what that was worth. But I was in no hurry to move on. I liked it here. I was beginning to understand why no one ever wanted to leave. But before I could be entirely at my ease, I really needed to pass my probation – and be sure that the school wasn't about to go bust.

* * *

I turned into the library, considering my plan for the afternoon. It had nothing to do with my classroom or the English curriculum, but everything to do with finding out more about the antique library books and what Mavis was doing with them. Mavis had gone to spend the weekend in Bath with her older sister, who lived in a retirement flat of which she was clearly envious.

Even Max had the weekend off as there were no girls on

site that needed his protection. His wife was also on leave. Rosemary had kindly invited me to help myself to any food I wanted from the kitchen over the weekend. So I was home alone. I should really have felt more nervous, especially without Max around, but after living in Steven's compact flat with him watching my every move, I was thrilled to have the sole run of such a huge space. I was tempted to do naughty things the girls weren't allowed to do, like slide down the bannisters and tap-dance on the dining tables. I held back only because if I fell off and injured myself, I'd have to wait a long time to be rescued.

The library seemed strangely empty without Mavis at the supervisor's desk. I sat in her seat for a moment to experience her perspective before moving to a round table in the corner, chosen for its proximity to a power point. I plugged in my laptop, turned it on, and brought up a website I'd found for valuing antique books. What treasures might I discover here this weekend?

I thought it best to work methodically, although Mavis had seemed to be picking books at random, judging from the scattered distribution of gaps. I drew a map of the library, one sheet of paper for each wall, and numbered the shelves. Then I set up a spreadsheet to allow me to enter the title, author, publisher, and year of publication for each book, against a reference number for its location.

Teetering up and down the library steps, I collected an armful of books and returned to my post. They were heavy, dusty, and fragile, and it took me five precarious trips up and down the ladder to decant a whole shelf. By my fifth descent, my thigh muscles were starting to object, and I was glad to sit down at my laptop.

I quickly realised this was no black-and-white matter: a book's condition could make a big difference to its price. Erring on the side of conservatism, I logged the lowest price that I could find for each.

The contents of this shelf alone, with its twenty-three books, was worth at least £1,000, even though to my layman's eyes none of them seemed particularly special. I glanced at my plan. Although two walls of the library were mostly windows, it still fitted about fifty high shelves containing the old books from Lord Bunting's days.

Picking up the first armful to replace, I glanced at the clock. Over an hour had flown by already. At this rate, there was no way I'd be able to value all the antique books on the shelves by the time everyone returned, or even a tiny fraction of them. As I climbed the steps again, I realised the massive scale of my undertaking. Country gentlemen used to employ young men (or women – Eve in Wodehouse's *Psmith*, again) for months at a time to catalogue their private libraries. And here was I thinking I could do it in twenty-four hours.

Still, if I managed to assess even a hundred books – my ambition was shrinking the more my aching thighs protested – the exercise would at least give me an idea of the library's total value and the scale of Mavis's profits, which would help me decide whether or not I should report her action to Miss Harnett and the bursar. Given that I'd just discovered a single shelf might be worth over a grand, it seems unlikely that Mavis was pocketing only the odd few quid. How low would the sum have to be for me to turn a blind eye? Knowing how destitute she would be without her job at St Bride's, I'd have to be very sure of my facts before turning her in.

The final volume on the next shelf changed my perspective, despite its tatty cover. How could a single book be worth £40,000? Because all the specialist websites I could find told me this one undoubtedly was.

29

HITTING THE JACKPOT

After returning the rest of its shelf-mates, I made a special trip up the steps to replace the very valuable book on its own, as fearful of dropping it as if it had been a Ming vase. I shelved it spine inwards, to make it easier to find again.

As I began my descent, I noticed the next shelf down held more volumes in the same series. A complete set would be worth much more.

I'd taken only a couple of steps down when the sound of the door opening made me jump. The steps wobbled, causing Joe to spot me straight away.

'Hello, you,' he called up cheerfully. 'That's a funny place to spend your exeat. Is that your idea of getting away from it all? Like one of those hermits in antiquity who lived on top of a pole to escape the temptations of the world?'

I forced a smile, realising how suspicious my behaviour looked.

Joe watched my every step as I descended.

'I might ask you the same question,' I said, hoping to

distract him. 'Why are you still here when I heard you telling Oriana you were cycling to Bristol to spend the weekend with friends? Did you change your mind?'

He wrinkled his nose. 'Problem with my brakes. Both cables had snapped. Can't think how. They were almost new. I hope it's not one of the girls playing a prank. They don't usually do that sort of thing. It could have been nasty.'

I bet no one would have interfered with his brake cables if Max had still been on site. Suddenly I felt very vulnerable. Who was left on campus to do such a thing? All the girls and the other staff had left for exeat, as far as I knew.

I reached the floor and dusted down my jeans.

'Why didn't you take one of your other bikes? It's not as if you haven't got a spare. Or fix it. You've got masses of bike parts in the shed.'

He shook his head. 'The others don't have racks for my panniers. I suppose I could have replaced the brake cables, but I'm not in the mood for faffing about and getting oily.'

He looked down at himself, and I realised this was only the second time I'd seen him in men's clothes – perfectly fitting jeans and, beneath a conker-brown leather jacket, a T-shirt stretched by taut muscle. I coughed.

'You could take Oriana's bike.'

'What, and risk looking like a girl?' He winked, making me realise how liberating exeats must be for him too. I noticed he hadn't shaved his face that morning. Blonde stubble was starting to show through. 'Nah. I thought I might catch Mavis before she left, hitch a lift with her to Bath, and get the train to Bristol from there, but she was off like a bullet from a starting pistol.'

'I thought starting pistols didn't have bullets?'

He grinned. 'Sorry. PE teacher's joke.'

'Yes, I saw her bombing up the drive, straight after the minibus.' I'd been careful to see her off the premises before I'd started my investigations.

He nodded. 'She's like a bat out of hell on exeats. Well, a panda out of hell, anyway. Fiat Panda. So what are your plans for the rest of the weekend?'

He followed me to my table. I quickly flipped my laptop shut and closed my notebook. Anyone seeing my spreadsheet might have thought it was me selling the library stock for my own gain, not Mavis. Bundling the laptop and notebook up under my arm, I hoped he wouldn't quiz me on what I'd been up to. Still unsure of his involvement in Mavis's little sideline, I didn't want to tell him.

'Oh, just a bit of catching up with myself. A bit of reading, a bit of marking, a bit of lesson planning.'

He frowned. 'Exeats are meant to be a break for staff as well as for pupils.'

'I've got some non-work emails to catch up with, too. I've sort of lost touch with my parents this year.'

The last four years, actually, but I was too ashamed to say it out loud.

'That'll hardly fill the weekend.' He glanced at the clock on the mantlepiece. 'Look, it's just about lunchtime. Come and have lunch with me. I'm a good cook. My omelettes are sublime.'

I was hungry, and I'd have to eat lunch sometime. Although a little nervous of spending the whole exeat with him, I now felt safer in his company than alone, given that whoever had doctored his brakes might have still been on campus. He seemed to sense me relenting.

'Come on, leave your stuff here. It'll be perfectly safe. I'll take you through the shortcut to the kitchen.'

So there were still parts of the school I hadn't seen? Another good reason to join him.

'Then afterwards how about we go for a walk? It's nice out now. Cold, but fresh. Get this library dust out of your lungs.'

It sounded like bliss.

30

IN THE FRAME

The concealed corridor behind the library marked what was once the start of the servants' quarters. Now it was lined with panoramic photos of the pupils taken throughout the school's history. In each one, the head, flanked by her staff, sat proudly at the centre of the first seated row, while the youngest girls knelt in front of them. Three rows of taller girls stood on benches behind the staff. The photos had been taken every seven years since St Bride's was founded back in 1897, to include all pupils who'd completed their education at the school.

I stopped to peer at each picture in turn. Each face was no bigger than a penny piece, but large enough to recognise. It was clear that most of the staff stayed at least seven years as they usually featured in more than one photo. I wondered how many photos would include me. I was already hoping I'd be here far longer than the year I'd planned as my springboard to escaping Steven, assuming I made it past my probationary period without issue.

'Only the last photo's worth spending any time over,' said Joe. 'Because that's the only one I'm in.'

He laid his hands lightly on my shoulders to steer me along to it.

After a few seconds' perusal, I put my finger on his tiny face in the photo, then wriggled free of his hands still on my shoulders to move back to the previous one.

'It's like travelling through time, don't you think?' I mused. 'I wonder how the teachers feel about having the evidence of their ageing process displayed for all to see?'

Joe grinned. 'Why do you think the photos have been relegated to this out-of-the-way corridor?'

I walked slowly back down the row of photos from newest to oldest, rejuvenating Miss Harnett by seven years with every shot until I reached the last picture to be taken before her appointment.

'She was beautiful when she was young, wasn't she? Very poised.'

Joe was standing in front of the second most recent photo. 'Look, and here's Oriana, looking as if she wants to be the next headmistress.'

I went to join him. 'Ooh, yes, and she's wearing glasses. I've never seen her in glasses before.'

'Probably fake glasses with plain lenses to try to make herself look clever.' Joe laughed. 'Either that or she was targeting some rich optician whose daughter had just joined the school. Still cute, though.'

I wandered back to the earlier photos, wondering how Joe felt about Oriana's new relationship with Steven. Jealous, I supposed. Although Mavis claimed Oriana had dumped Joe, there still seemed to be a spark between them.

I sighed. Just my luck to discover the only eligible man in the place was besotted with someone else. And the bursar was, too, though he clearly didn't stand a chance with her.

Then Joe put his hand on the small of my back to coax me along.

'Come on, then, my time-travelling friend. Let's take the Tardis back to lunchtime. I'm starving.'

* * *

Joe was right. His omelette was sublime. I'd expected him, as a former professional athlete used to carb-loading, to rustle up something stodgy, but his creation was feather-light and subtle. He whipped egg whites to stiff peaks before folding them into beaten yolks, then tipped them into a pan of sizzling butter, delicately snipped fresh chives and parsley from the kitchen window box, scattered them across the slowly setting surface and ground on a hint of sea salt. His hands, like the rest of him, may have been firm and muscular, but they were sensitive too.

'That looks delicious,' I said, as he flipped the omelette closed and slipped it on to a serving dish.

He grinned. 'You haven't tasted it yet.'

We sat in the small anteroom of the kitchen where the domestic staff usually ate.

'It's such a treat to be cooked for,' I said after savouring the first mouthful, which tasted even better than it looked.

Joe picked up his knife and fork. 'You've had meals cooked for you all term.'

I couldn't resist another mouthful before replying.

'I mean by a man. Steven never cooked a thing. I did it all. And the washing up. Not that I minded. It was one area where I wanted to be in charge.'

Joe tried to sound casual. 'I hear Steven's cooking for Oriana this weekend.' Aware he was watching me, I focused on my plate. 'Bet he's not as good a cook as I am, Gemma.'

I looked up. 'You're worried about the competition?'

'Competition is my middle name. You don't get far in the world of cycling without it.'

I welcomed the chance to find out more about his former career – and to steer the conversation away from Steven.

'So how far did you get?'

His turn to look away. 'Far enough. And now I can't get far enough away from it.'

'Why would you want to? It sounds like an exciting life. Assuming you retired for medical reasons, weren't you tempted to stay in the same world and become a sports coach or a commentator? You've the aptitude to do either of those things, from what I've seen of you so far.'

He hesitated. 'Professional cycling is a claustrophobic world.'

'And boarding school life isn't?'

'That's different. Besides, it's not like the experience was wasted. I can apply skills I've learned in my sporting career here. Staying power, positive thinking, and determination, quite apart from physical sports techniques.'

There was an edge in his voice, as if he didn't believe his own words, so I decided not to press him any further.

We ate the rest of the omelette in silence, then I took the plates and cutlery to the small sink in the corner of the room to wash them, ignoring the industrial-sized dishwasher that lay empty in the scullery next door.

Joe picked up a tea towel to dry them.

'So, what next, Miss Lamb? Back to your dusty pursuits in the library? You're brave, treading on Miss Brook's territory.'

'I'm only valuing the books, not selling them.'

It slipped out before I realised he'd been referring only to my presence in the library, not to what I was doing there. He stared at me for a moment, leaving me unsure whether he knew what I was talking about.

'An English teacher who did not value books would not be much of an English teacher,' he said at last, standing up. 'Come on, let's go for that walk.'

After collecting our coats from our flats, we met back at the library, entering the rear gardens via the heavy French doors. The chilly air in the weak afternoon sunshine made me gasp, and Joe laughed.

'You wimp! You're as bad as the girls. Come on, a bit of outdoor oxygen will do you good. You'll soon warm up once we get moving. Let's go down to the lake.'

The lake lay a few minutes' walk away, beyond the mausoleum. As we approached, Joe pulled from his jacket pocket a paper bag of stale bread.

'Look what I liberated from the kitchen.' He smiled, holding the bag open for me to help myself.

I rummaged inside to grab a handful, my fingers brushing

against Joe's palm through the paper. Even in this cold air, his hands were warm. All that cycling must have boosted his circulation permanently.

The school swans flocked towards us as we approached the lake, Joe following a couple of steps behind me.

'You know we're about to break school rules?'

I wondered what he thought we were about to do.

'Feeding the swans, I mean. The girls aren't allowed to, or the swans would soon be fit to burst.'

We watched the big white birds gobble up every last scrap, including the stray crumbs Joe shook from the bag. He returned it to his pocket as they were threatening to snaffle the bag too. Standing still for so long in the damp lakeside air, I began to feel the cold, and I shivered, wrapping my arms about my body for warmth. When Joe rested a hand on my shoulder, it felt like he'd applied a hot-water bottle.

'How about we go back inside and watch a film? There are tons of DVDs in the girls' common rooms, and not all of them are dreadful. You can choose.'

I beamed. Next, he'd be giving me control of the remote. I'd never had the chance to learn how to use Steven's. What had I been thinking to put up with him for so long?

* * *

In the Poorhouse common room, I slipped *The African Queen* into the DVD player and was about to sit in the armchair beside the sofa, where Joe had installed himself, when he reached out a hand to me.

'Come on, you can sit next to me, I won't bite. Not unless you want me to.'

Just then, the common room door flew open, making us both jump.

'Well, this is cosy,' snapped Oriana, storming in and flinging herself down in the centre of the sofa where I'd been about to sit. Joe immediately shrank back, withdrawing his arm from where he'd laid it along the back of the sofa. He crossed his legs away from her, and I made for the armchair.

'Oriana, you're back!' I said.

She folded her arms. 'Well, obviously.'

'Lover boy stood you up?' said Joe tersely, before turning to me. I suspected he might have been jealous. 'Sorry, Gemma.'

'What are you apologising to her for? It's me that's been slighted.'

'Slighted? How? What did he do?' I asked.

My stomach churned at the thought of what harm Steven might have done to her.

She pouted. 'Honestly, Gemma, you might have warned me.'

'I did tell you he was controlling,' I faltered, dreading what she might say next.

She kicked off her shoes and rested her feet on the coffee table.

'Who's talking about control? I thought you said he was well off.' She picked at her immaculate nails. 'But his supposed apartment was barely bigger than a bedsit. And the furniture! Flat-pack, every last piece of it: shiny, new, and soulless.'

I was so relieved I almost laughed aloud.

'Sorry, Oriana, Steven doesn't like second-hand stuff. He thinks it's demeaning. Not that I agree with him.'

I patted the old armchair affectionately.

Oriana rolled her eyes. 'Second-hand? *Second-hand?* Oh, God forbid one might soil one's apartment' – she said the word sarcastically – 'with antiques or family heirlooms. No, much better to have cheap plastic stuff turned out by the gazillion to be just the same as everyone else's.' She picked up a faded needlepoint scatter cushion, the work of a former housemistress, and hugged it to her chest. 'Oh yes, give me nylon and MDF any day. Not.'

'He prides himself on buying everything new. He thinks it demonstrates how well he's doing for himself – that he's got a good job.'

Oriana punched the cushion. 'Not that good a job. I thought from his car that he was seriously rich. Not *IKEA* rich.'

Joe smirked. 'And that matters because?'

She bashed him over the head with her cushion, then flung it on his lap.

'Oh Joe, don't be so mean. You know the type I go for.'

Then she turned to me. 'Honestly, Gemma, you might have told me that man's a fraud, driving a flash car like that when his flat's no bigger than mine.'

Joe winked at me. 'Size isn't everything, is it, Gemma?'

Oriana swivelled round to look daggers at him. 'Well, you should know.' She stalked across to perch on the arm of my chair.

'It's a nice enough flat,' I protested. 'In a convenient position, with its own off-street parking.'

'What are you now, his estate agent?'

Her anger trumped her usually good manners.

'It's a bachelor flat and he's a bachelor.' I didn't know why I was defending him.

'Yes, but it's hardly the residential equivalent of the car he drives. I thought it would have to be a penthouse at least. And have furniture passed down by his family.'

In principle, I agreed with her. I had been horrified when Steven announced he was spending the equivalent of a deposit on a house on his new car. After all, I'd told him, you spend a lot more time in your home than in your car. Wouldn't that money be better spent upgrading your flat?

Steven had been unbending. 'My parents think it's a great idea. My dad said he was proud to have a son driving a car like that.'

And therein lay the problem: Steven's parents, who, if offered the gift of the Midas touch, would seize it with both hands.

Oriana got to her feet, brushed herself down, and straightened her skirt. 'Now I'm off to have a shower to slough off the whole experience. I'll see you in the kitchen at suppertime, if you're dining in.'

After giving a silent wave, Joe turned his attention to the television screen. I sank back in my armchair and pressed play.

31

FALLEN FLAT

It was a solemn supper the three of us shared in the kitchen, the mood so different from my lunch with Joe. I cooked spaghetti carbonara, which settled heavily in my stomach as afterwards we sprawled in the Poorhouse common room. Oriana had rallied after her shower, and she and Joe idly fired flirtatious banter back and forth. They sat on the sofa while I curled up in my armchair feeling like a bloated gooseberry. Flicking through the television channels, failing to find something we all wanted to watch, I almost excused myself to resume my investigations in the library, but was wary of leaving them alone together in case Oriana sought consolation from Joe for her failed date with Steven.

She seemed unable to drop the subject, running Steven down so harshly for his taste in interior decor that even Joe ended up accidentally defending him.

'I'm sure Steven didn't mean to mislead you. Poor sap probably thought you liked him for himself. Or at least for his car.' Joe jabbed her arm teasingly with his forefinger. 'Or maybe he was playing you at your own game. He might have thought St Bride's was your private house and you either owned the estate or were heiress to it. That would make you a valuable catch.'

She pushed his finger away. 'Hardly. He knew it was a school and came here because he knew Gemma had got a job here. What's more, he spotted Gemma's car on the forecourt the first time he visited.' I covered my face with my hands. Of course he would have seen my car! How could I have been so stupid? 'He didn't really fall for the wild goose chase I tried to send him on to Wendlebury Barrow. Although if he was a gold digger, the selfie I sent him after our first meeting would not have helped.'

Joe raised a quizzical eyebrow. 'Oh, Oriana, you little minx!'

She shot him a disgusted look. 'No, not that sort of selfie, you filthy beast. One of me fully dressed and entirely respectable, relaxing elegantly in my school flat.'

Joe clapped a hand over his mouth to suppress his laughter.

'With a backdrop of Bolivars? You idiot! No wonder he asked you out!'

Oriana turned to me for support.

'But you'd told me he was a merchant banker. Surely he'd know they were worthless?'

I tried not to enjoy Steven's comeuppance.

'Yes, but his speciality is European currencies. He'll have heard of the Bolivar crisis, but he wouldn't necessarily recognise one on the wall in the background of a selfie.' I bit my lip. 'Besides, even Steven would focus on you rather than the wallpaper. You're much prettier.'

Oriana pursed her lips. 'I don't think he thought about me at all, if you must know.' She turned to me accusingly. 'His flat was still full of pictures of you, Gemma.'

Honestly, her powers of exaggeration were worse than the girls' tall tales.

'Really?' The only photo of me I remembered being on display was taken at one of Steven's corporate dinners, at which he was receiving a banking industry award. He was quick to get that one framed, unlike our many holiday photos that never made it off the memory card of his camera.

Oriana scowled. 'You'd think as a matter of courtesy he might have taken them down before my visit. It was the numerous photos of you on display that made me realise he wasn't actually interested in me at all.'

I was about to ask more about those photos, then I realised I didn't really want to know. The thought of Steven obsessing about me made me feel queasy. I was just glad that Oriana's relationship with Steven had ended so quickly without her coming to any harm.

'Anyway, I've given him his marching orders,' continued Oriana. 'I've forbidden him ever to darken the doorstep of St Bride's School ever again. I'm going to tell Max to ban him from the premises.'

It was about time someone did.

But I couldn't bear to think of Steven any longer. Hoping a DVD might divert us all, I got up to look for one on the shelf. 'What shall we watch?'

Joe smirked. 'How about *Some Like It Hot*?'

'Joe, you are as subtle as a... as a...' Oriana fizzled out, twisting round to lie full length on the sofa with her feet on

Joe's lap. Gently he slipped off her shoes and set them on the floor before resting his hands on her stockinged feet. Perhaps he was happy to serve as her consolation prize between other men, like a palate cleanser between courses. Some girls have all the luck.

I'd have chosen *Cabaret*, one of my all-time favourite films, had it been there, which of course it wasn't, being unsuitable for under-eighteens. Surely Sally Bowles was the role Oriana was born to play? Instead, feeling every inch the English teacher, I selected the BBC *Pride and Prejudice* series starring Colin Firth, and settled down in my armchair with my back to the pair of them, trying not to feel left out.

32

GLOOMY SUNDAY

After the unexpected events of Saturday, I appeared to be back in isolation the next morning. Taking Joe's secret route to the kitchen in search of breakfast, I thought I might bump into him on the way, though not necessarily into Oriana. I hoped he might have ideas for something we could all do together until the girls returned. I felt duty-bound to return to my research in the library, but those few hours I'd spent alone with Joe the previous afternoon had made me hanker after more leisure time with him.

Not that I was ready to start a new relationship so soon after leaving Steven. The whole point of my coming here had been to avoid men for a while. But spending time with a courteous, kind man was reminding me of just how pleasant it was to be in a proper grown-up relationship of equals. I had missed that for so long. I hoped Oriana, now shot of Steven, might soon find someone similar for herself too. In any case, I vowed I'd never allow myself to be so cowed by a boyfriend again.

As I finished my tea and toast, I contemplated knocking on the door of Joe's flat over in the Doghouse, to ask whether he'd like to go for a walk, or perhaps cycle together to the nearest pub, The Bluebird in Wendlebury Barrow, for Sunday lunch. However, after last night's display of his physical closeness with Oriana, I wasn't entirely confident that I wouldn't find her in his room, or vice versa, after spending the night there. That would be embarrassing for me at least, although they would probably brazen it out. They might have even assumed I knew that would happen. They had an easy, confident familiarity with each other, the kind I'd never enjoyed with Steven.

I began to wonder whether Oriana's games with the girls' fathers were simply a bit of idle fun, designed to milk them for what she could materially, before she returned in between times to the comforts of penniless Joe.

So it was back to the library alone for me. Knowing others were in the building now, I wasn't keen to work as openly as I had planned. However, I did want to see whether I could find any more very valuable books.

The library steps were where I'd left them, and I ascended to where I'd stashed the special book, easy to spot with its spine turned inwards. I decided to examine as many of the other books in the same series as I could squeeze into the limited time left to me. The best way forward would be to handle just one book at a time, in case they were equally valuable. Dropping one from the top of the ladder could knock thousands off its worth. With the next book tucked under my arm, I glanced at the ground and gulped. Such a fall wouldn't do me any good either.

Behind me, a door creaked open and the ladder wobbled

slightly. Hanging on to the post at the top, I turned my head, hoping to see Joe coming in search of me.

It was Oriana.

'Oh, you're in here, Gemma. I'm looking for Joe.'

I didn't reply till I'd climbed down to her level and one foot had touched the welcome solidity of the parquet floor.

'No, sorry, I haven't seen Joe this morning.'

Oriana brightened. 'Off on his bike somewhere, I expect. He likes to take off on long rides when the girls aren't here, so he can go at full pelt without them watching.'

I set the book face down on the table to obscure what I was doing, but Oriana wasn't interested in books.

'Why wouldn't he want them to see how fast he can go? Surely they'd be impressed and inspired in their own sporting endeavours?'

Joe was right: I really did sound like a school prospectus sometimes.

Oriana settled down in the chair opposite mine, clasped her hands, and peered at me beneath the green glass lamp suspended on brass chains above our heads.

'Isn't that obvious? They're not meant to know how distinguished his sporting past was. That he competed at international level. And that he can cycle faster than any woman.'

She paused for a moment, and I realised there was something she wasn't telling me.

'All this subterfuge seems like very hard work for Joe, let alone the school,' I said. 'Why didn't the headmistress just employ a woman in the first place? I can't imagine there'd be a shortage of female PE teachers who'd be glad to work in a place like this. How many other schools have such huge, beautiful grounds, with so much space available for sport?'

Oriana leaned back in her chair, rested her elbows on its curving wooden arms, and looked away from me, out of the window.

'Oh, Hairnet had her reasons,' she said. 'Anyway, enough about Joe. What are you doing today?'

I patted the copy of *Pride and Prejudice* I'd brought with me from my room.

'Just catching up on a bit of reading.' I indicated the squashy leather Chesterfield in the bay window. 'There's better light here for reading than in my flat.'

She stared in dismay at the cover. 'What, that old thing again? But you only watched the TV series last night!' She got to her feet. 'I'm off to Slate Green for the Sunday papers. I'll be reading them in the staffroom, so I can spread them out on the big table. Come and join me if you want something interesting to read. I'll charge up Old Faithful when I get back to keep us going till the girls return. Otherwise, I'll meet you for lunch in the kitchen. One o'clock suit you?'

I nodded. 'Yes, thanks.'

'There's a decent quiche and some salad in the fridge. And some leftover apple pie from supper on Friday.'

'Fine.' I forced a smile and picked up my novel, but as soon as she left, I put it back in my bag and fired up my laptop. Perhaps our lunch together would provide the opportunity I needed to tell her about Mavis's secret scam. Perhaps Oriana, and Joe, assuming he was back in time, could advise me on how best to alert the bursar and Hairnet to the true worth of the books she was surreptitiously selling off, without Mavis losing her job or even ending up in prison. Despite her needing employment and a flat as much as I did, I couldn't stay silent about the true worth of the valuable books I had discovered, knowing they might save the school.

But Oriana wasn't in the kitchen when I got there at 1 p.m., and nor was Joe. I pulled my phone out of my pocket to see whether she'd texted me with a change of plan but there were no new messages.

I played for time by setting the table for the three of us, slicing fresh salad vegetables and arranging them in serving dishes, and warming the quiche in the oven. By the time it was heated, neither Joe nor Oriana had arrived, and I was hungry, so I helped myself, eating slowly as I listened for footsteps. None came.

Perhaps Oriana had tracked down Joe after all. Perhaps they were at this very minute savouring a lovely Sunday roast at The Bluebird. For a moment I considered abandoning the quiche and jumping in my car to go and look for them. But I didn't want to find them enjoying a tête-à-tête.

Then I thought about bypassing the pub and heading for the bookshop – Hector's House, I'd learned it was called. Perhaps Hector might give me his verdict on the precious book I'd found. On my phone, I searched for the Hector's House website and was disappointed to discover the shop didn't open on Sundays.

I cut myself a second slice of quiche as compensation.

By the time I'd washed up my plate and cutlery and left the kitchen as I'd found it, it was nearly 2 p.m. Just a couple of hours of privacy remained before the staff returned, and a further four before the girls were due back. Realising I hadn't been outside for nearly twenty-four hours, I decided some fresh air might cheer me up.

Collecting my coat from my flat and pocketing a couple of biscuits to feed the swans, I paused to listen at Oriana's door for evidence of activity. It was as silent as the mausoleum.

I headed for the lake, retracing my steps from yesterday's walk with Joe. But even the swans had abandoned me, as if they too were on exeat. For a little while, I sat on the bench where I'd lingered with Joe at the water's edge. Golden and scarlet leaves were drifting gently from the surrounding trees on to the lake's surface. I wished I'd brought my book, although I wasn't really in the mood for reading. Idly I nibbled one of the biscuits.

I wasn't ready to return to the library either. Perhaps staying in school for the weekend had been a mistake. I was starting to feel stir-crazy. Apart from the outing to the bookshop with Joe, I'd not left the school grounds since the first day of term. That didn't seem very healthy, but I'd left it too late to go out now. By the time I got anywhere worthwhile, it would be time to come back.

What else might I do that was stimulating without leaving the school grounds? Where might I find fresh inspiration?

I thought of Miss Harnett and Lord Bunting. Crumbling the rest of my biscuit on to the grass for an optimistic robin hopping about my feet, I got up from the bench and headed for the mausoleum.

33

COLD SHOULDER

I heaved open the porch door and entered the mausoleum. For a moment I thought I heard a faint cry, but once I was inside, the silence hit me like a wall. It was even quieter than the empty school building. I'd been surprised that I'd been missing the sound of the school bells, which didn't ring during exeat weekends.

As I pushed aside the inner velvet curtain, I wondered how many staff continued to operate to the school's daily timetable outside of term time. Judith Gosling had shown me a series of alarms on her mobile phone set to synchronise with the school bell system. I wondered whether she let it run during the holidays.

I blinked a few times to adjust to the dim light, wandering slowly around the corner towards the stained-glass windows. It wasn't that bright outside, but now my eyes seemed to be playing tricks on me. I blinked some more, not believing what I saw on the second plinth, and walked slowly and cautiously towards it, although my heart was pounding as if I was running full pelt. For there, arranged as neatly as Lord Bunting's effigy opposite, was someone that looked exactly like me, lying on the plinth as if, at first glance, in quiet contemplation. Perhaps Miss Harnett was not the only one who liked to do so. But if that's what this person had come here for, her plan had gone wildly wrong. On closer inspection, she did not look in the least serene, but was puffy of face, lips open and gasping, her airways restricted by something dark and shining around her neck.

A shaft of sunshine broke through the clouds, beaming down through the windows like a kaleidoscopic torch upon her face, *Oriana's* face, framed by her hair done in imitation of mine, flowing down over a plain, modest T-shirt that could have come straight out of my wardrobe. I glanced at her chest – still rising and falling, though in awkward jerks. I stumbled as I broke into a run to be at her side, grabbing with both hands at the rubber strip around her neck. I half-expected her to slap my hands away for interfering, until I realised she was out cold, her hands limp by her sides.

The rubber clung to my hands as I struggled to remove it. It hadn't been as tight as I'd feared, and as soon as I pulled it free, Oriana started to come round, drawing a desperate, deep, and noisy breath to refill her strained lungs. Her eyelids flickered without opening, and her hands fluttered to clutch her throat. Thank goodness she was still very much alive.

Selfishly relieved that I wouldn't have to attempt mouth-to-mouth resuscitation, I was at a loss as to what to do next. I looked down at the loop of rubber in my hand. Was it strong enough to have broken her neck? If so, I shouldn't move her. She needed professional medical help. I slipped off my coat, tucked it over her chilled body, murmured the first words of comfort that occurred to me, and pulled my phone from my jeans pocket to call an ambulance.

Drat! No reception! The walls of this ancient building were too thick for a phone signal to penetrate.

'I'll be right back, Oriana, I promise,' I called to her, wishing my voice wasn't so tremulous as I dashed outside to make the call.

I ran out on to the lawn, waving my phone above my head to get a signal.

With the ambulance on its way, I turned to go back to the mausoleum to comfort Oriana until it arrived. For the first time, I spotted Joe's racing bike, flung against the wall of the yard, with one wheel wrenched from its axis and the tyre split open. I became conscious of the cold, clammy strip of stuff still dangling in my hand: the circle of rubber I'd removed from Oriana's neck was the inner tube of a bicycle tyre.

Joe was nowhere to be seen.

With a gasp, I dropped the inner tube on the ground, then picked it up again. It must not get lost. It would be important evidence for the paramedics attending to Oriana's injury, and the police who now must surely be called to investigate the assault.

But Joe – why Joe? My heart sank at my failure, yet again, to judge a man's character. I liked him very much, but had noticed how tactile he was, always touching people. Perhaps a hands-on attack like this might have been just his style. But what on earth would drive him to do something so dreadful, and to someone with whom he seemed to have such a rapport?

I pulled myself together. Now was not the time to play detective. My immediate priority was to help Oriana recover. I dashed back into the mausoleum where I found her still breathing, but it worried me that she wasn't trying to communicate. Oriana was not the kind to suffer in silence. Her forehead was cold. I looked about for something more to warm her. I grabbed the pole above the porch door, wrenched it down from its bracket, and slid the velvet curtain off on to the floor, scattering brass rings all around me. It was heavier than it looked, so I dragged rather than carried it to the second plinth where I draped it over Oriana's whole body, right up to her chin.

The puffiness in her face was beginning to subside. With her hair splayed out about her face like a sunburst, she reminded me of Sleeping Beauty awaiting a kiss from her handsome prince. All that was missing was the glass case. And the prince. I reached underneath for one of her hands to hold for comfort and was relieved when she returned a faint pressure.

Not knowing what else to do, I started to talk to her. I'd recently overheard Dr Fielding saying in the staffroom that when you're dying, your sense of hearing is the last to go. I didn't think Oriana was dying, but I felt I ought to talk to her all the same.

'Don't worry, Oriana, you'll be fine,' I began. 'I've called the emergency services and an ambulance will be here soon. They're sending a police car too. I'm sure the damage is only superficial. Just get your breath back and rest. Don't move. Think calm thoughts. Try to think of kittens—'

I'd have wittered on till the ambulance arrived had I not

been startled half out of my wits, or what was left of them, by the sound of a door being flung open with such force that it crashed against the wall. For one terrifying moment, I feared the return of Oriana's assailant. Had he mistaken her for me, only realising his mistake when I turned up? My heart nearly burst out of my chest, and I wondered whether the paramedics would have room in the ambulance for a second casualty.

'Max, for goodness' sake, you frightened the life out of me!'

Because it was Max, inadvertently demonstrating his muscle power.

'I told you I was only ever a scream away,' he said, dusting himself down as he strode towards us.

He bent over Oriana, placed his fingers on the pulse in her neck, and listened to her breathing, nodding with satisfaction at the evenness beneath the still rasping tone. Then, ever so gently, he pulled down the neck of her T-shirt to inspect the red weal without touching it.

I held up the inner tube. 'I found this wrapped round her neck. She was choking.'

Max tutted. 'Bloody amateur. If you really want to garrotte someone, use something that doesn't stretch.'

A chill ran through me. 'If I really want? Surely you don't think I did it! No, of course you don't. Sorry, Max, I'm being ridiculous.'

Max glanced about us. 'Did you find anything else incriminating?'

'Like the rest of the bicycle?' I hesitated. 'Yes. It's one of Joe's. It's lying against the far outside wall of the mausoleum. One of its wheels has been wrenched off to remove an inner tube.'

Max frowned. 'Joe would never treat his precious bike like that.'

Typical man! How could he think about the bike at a time like this? 'What about Oriana?'

'Nor would Oriana,' he went on. 'Besides, why go to the trouble of ripping out a perfectly good inner tube from a wheel, if you've got one sitting unused in a cardboard box?'

'But who else could it be?' I asked. 'There's hardly anyone on site, apart from us and the bursar and possibly Miss Harnett. Everyone else has gone away for exeat. Unless there was an intruder. But you'd have seen any intruders and stopped them, right?'

Max blanched.

'Remember, Gemma, I'm off duty during exeats. I only come back on when the staff return. I have to have some time with my wife, you know. Fortunately the sound monitor in my house picked up two screams here, first a woman's, then a man's, so I ran here as fast as I could.'

He marched across to the cupboard door, opened it, and peered inside before slamming it closed. He turned the key in the lock and slipped it into one of his many pockets.

'Whoever he is, he can't have got far. I'll find him before he can harm anyone else, don't you worry.'

I gave a sigh of relief. 'I'll stay with Oriana till the emergency services get here, if you go and look for the intruder.'

He nodded, keen to begin his search.

As he opened the porch door, a yell of rage resounded from outside.

'Who the hell's been vandalising my best racing bike?'

If Joe was attempting to cover up for his own misdemeanour, he was making a convincing job of it.

Max left the door wide open behind him, which made me feel a little safer as I resumed offering words of comfort to Oriana. As I spoke, I strained to hear the rapid exchange of words between Joe and Max but I couldn't make any sense of them. Then one of them ran away up the path, judging by the sound of gravel crunching underfoot.

It must have been Max, as suddenly Joe was standing there facing me in the mausoleum. As soon as he saw Oriana unconscious on the plinth and me leaning over her, he rushed up the aisle.

'Gemma, what's happened to Oriana? Are you okay? What's going on? I was just going down to look for you by the lake and I saw my bike in pieces beside the porch, then Max came charging out and told me to come in and take care of you both.'

I didn't want to speak aloud about Oriana's injuries for fear of frightening her, if she could hear me. So I just let go of her hands and held up the inner tube to show Joe. Then I drew a finger across my throat to indicate the damage.

'Oh my goodness!' said Joe. 'Who would do a thing like that to her of all people? No, wait, I can think of a few.'

My eyes widened in wonder. Not the bursar, surely? Perhaps he was jealous of her new relationship with Steven.

'But don't worry about Oriana,' Joe went on. 'She'll be fine. Though her frame may be slight, it's as resilient as a mountain bike.'

Oriana's eyelids flickered, and she tried to raise herself up on her elbows, but couldn't muster the strength. 'Oh, thanks a lot, Joe.' Her voice was hoarse and low. 'Don't come to me for sympathy next time you fall off your bike.'

'I never fall off my bike,' retorted Joe. 'And it would take a lot more than a bit of rubber to fell me.'

'I could beat you at arm wrestling any day.' She reached out a lean, well-toned arm and then slid it back slightly, startled by how weak she'd become.

'Let's save that for another day,' said Joe. 'For now, just tell me who on earth did this to you.'

'Who do you bloody think?' said Oriana, lying back and pulling the curtain up to her neck for warmth. 'You think I found out Max's true identity, so he had to kill me?'

I hadn't thought of that.

Joe bent to inspect the damage to her throat. 'No, Max would have done a more professional job of it. This is the work of an amateur,' he said.

'You can say that again.' Oriana snapped her head round to glare at me, then groaned with pain at having moved her injured neck too fast. 'This is all your fault, Gemma.'

'What?' I recoiled a few steps in horror until my back was pressed against Lord Bunting. 'Oh no! Don't tell me it was Steven!'

'Yes, it was your bloody boyfriend Steven. He must have sneaked into the grounds this afternoon when Max was off guard and lurked about waiting to find you.'

'To find me? Surely it wasn't me he wanted?'

'In the dim light in here, he mistook me for you.'

'But he wouldn't do anything like this. He never did when we were together.'

'Doesn't mean he's not capable.' Joe spoke softly. 'Besides, that's not quite the truth, is it, Gemma? Don't think I didn't notice those marks on your wrists at the start of term.'

I tucked my hands and wrists under my armpits to hide any remaining evidence of bruising.

Oriana was rallying now. 'Anyway, I called his bluff and played dead to frighten him, the cowardly little runt. But here's the important thing: he called me your name as he crept up behind me and put that evil rubber thing around my neck. I don't think you realise how angry you made him when you left, Gemma. He's not over you yet, you know. Far from it.'

'But he moved straight on to you, didn't he?'

'Only because he thought I was a means of getting back to you. At first he wanted me to be his emissary, to persuade you to return to him, but I wasn't prepared to be strung along for his own ends. Now it seems that he decided that if he couldn't have you, no one else would, and attacked me, thinking I was you. What a nasty piece of work. Whatever did you see in him, Gemma?'

Same as you, I wanted to say. Superficial charm, good looks, a well-paid career. But that wasn't enough.

Oriana sighed. 'Actually, I don't think I was ever truly in any danger. I know enough about self-defence to send any man packing with a single blow of my high heels.'

'Then why didn't you?' I said gently.

Joe frowned. 'It's true, Gemma, usually she could fell a sumo wrestler with an artful aim of her heel. Haven't you seen how she strides about the place? Her leg muscles are second only to mine.'

I glanced at her toes, sticking out from beneath the curtain. 'Except lately she's been wearing sensible flatties like mine.' I bent to retrieve them from the floor and set them on the plinth by her feet.

Oriana stared at them, open-mouthed. 'You're right. Oh well, all's well that ends well.'

And with that she fainted.

At that point the door creaked open to admit the bursar, rushing in ahead of a pair of paramedics.

'Oriana, darling!'

As he wrapped his arms around her, she revived, and though her eyes remained closed, she batted him away with a sturdy punch to his chest.

The bursar clasped the hand that had punched him.

'Max just told me you'd been attacked. My poor angel!'

'Oh, for goodness' sake, Bursar, I'm fine. If you want to make yourself useful, go and get my mum.' Her lower lip began to quiver. 'I want my mum.'

The bursar backed away, genuinely distraught, then scuttled off to who knew where to carry out Oriana's request, almost falling over McPhee on his way out.

With the self-assurance that only a cat can muster, McPhee trotted up to the plinth before leaping elegantly up to stand at Oriana's side, rubbing his face against her cheek, purring loudly. Oriana reached out with both arms to clasp the cat to her chest and began to sob quietly into his soft fur.

Setting down their bags beside the plinth, the paramedics gently worked around McPhee to check Oriana's vital signs. Meanwhile I let Joe wrap his arms around me to keep me upright as I told them what I could about Oriana's ordeal.

34

TUNNEL VISION

'If Steven wanted to kill Gemma, you'd think he could have found an easier way.'

Sitting on the sofa in the head's study, I took a sip from the mug of cocoa that the bursar had pressed into my hand.

'I mean,' I continued, 'he might have brought a more conventional weapon with him rather than depending on a handy bike to be about the place, from which to extract an inner tube. He never did like getting his hands dirty.'

'Oh, but isn't it obvious?' said the bursar. 'Of course he didn't want to kill Oriana. He just wanted to frame Joe. That's why he vandalised Joe's bike: to create an incriminating weapon. Must have been jealous of your new relationship with him.'

'My new relationship?' I glanced at Joe to see what he made of the bursar's theory, but he was staring into his mug, giving nothing away. 'I mean, we're friends, of course, but—'

'Oh, for heaven's sake, girl, are you the only one who hasn't noticed him making sheep's eyes at you?' said the bursar.

Joe looked up, giving me an unusually shy smile. I blushed and looked away as he began to speak.

'Oriana confided in me last week that she'd told Steven you had started a new relationship with me. She hoped that would make him think you'd moved on. Then she could have him for herself.'

Oriana wasn't there to verify the bursar's theory, nor to contradict Joe, having been taken off to hospital to make sure the damage to her throat was only superficial.

'How helpful of her,' I said tersely.

'Still, that doesn't excuse him from ripping out my inner tube to attempt murder!' said Joe. Then he clapped his hand to his mouth in sudden realisation. 'Do you know what, Gemma? I bet it was Steven who cut my brake cables yesterday.'

That made sense. If Steven was capable of attempting to strangle someone with an inner tube to get his own way, he wouldn't think twice about sabotaging the brakes of a bicycle. I sat up straight, adrenaline surging through my veins.

'But if everyone is so sure it was Steven, where is he now? We're all accusing him, but he's nowhere to be found. Presumably the police will check the inner tube for fingerprints and DNA though – provided I haven't covered them all up with mine.'

I was kicking myself for being so stupid as to handle the wretched thing.

'You're forgetting our secret weapon: Max Security,' said the bursar.

I gave a hollow laugh. 'If Max was that smart, he'd have stopped Steven entering the grounds in the first place, and no harm would have been done. Or at the very least he'd have captured him on one of his surveillance cameras.'

The bursar stared at the ground. 'It's his weekend off, Gemma. Everybody has to have a break sometime.'

I sighed. 'Of course, Max must have his time off, just the same as the rest of us. But if I hadn't walked into the mausoleum when I did, Oriana might have died. Steven – or the attacker, whoever it was, if Oriana is mistaken – must have fled when he heard me opening the door. That heavy old door is slow to open, then you have to get past that ridiculous curtain. He'd have had a few seconds to make himself scarce.'

'But he'd have had to pass you in the doorway to get out,' said Joe.

'Then perhaps he was there all along, hiding behind Lord Bunting's plinth. After all, there aren't many places in there that you can hide.' I shivered. 'Unless he knew about the secret entrance to the tunnel system, hidden by the cupboard doors. Either way, I'm lucky he didn't leap out and attack me too.'

Joe laid a comforting hand on my shoulder.

'But he didn't, and you're okay.'

'You really don't need to worry any more, Gemma,' said the bursar. 'He won't allow Steven a second chance at harm. He'll be on the case, you'll see.'

Joe stood up and set his empty cocoa mug on the coffee table. 'Speak of the devil, here he comes now. And he's got company.'

Joe and the bursar crossed to the big bay window which overlooked the lawns. When I went to join them, I was astonished to see Max frogmarching a handcuffed Steven up from the mausoleum towards us. The bursar heaved up one of the big sash windows and we all leaned out.

'Where did you find this specimen?' asked Joe.

Max grinned.

'Apparently when he heard you opening the mausoleum door, he hid in the cupboard without realising it was the entrance to a tunnel. In the dark, he fell down the steps and thought he'd stumbled upon a sneaky escape route, but the other end of the tunnel comes up in the middle of my lawn. I had an idea that might be where he'd gone. You'll remember I locked the cupboard door, Gemma? Then when I left you at the mausoleum, I ran back to my house just in time to see Steven emerge like a mole from a molehill. Then I nabbed him.'

Steven tried to pull away from Max, twisting about so as not to face me, but Max yanked at the handcuffs to make him stay still.

'As soon as he saw me, he did a quick about-turn, thinking there might be another way out of the tunnel. I slammed the hatch down and locked it, knowing that the only other exit was back in the mausoleum. Sprinting above ground when he could only crawl below, I got there before he did, and was standing at the cupboard door to meet him, handcuffs at the ready.'

'This place is a madhouse,' cried Steven. 'I'll have you all done for assault and unlawful imprisonment.' He raised his cuffed hands and shook them in the direction of Joe. 'And I don't know what you're wasting your time with him for, Gemma. Don't you know who he is? He's a convicted fraudster and a cheat.'

Joe turned appealing eyes on me. 'Honestly, Gemma, I can explain.'

Before I could manage a reply, Max gave the handcuffs another tug and marched Steven away, around the side of the house to the car park, where a brief burst of sirens in the distance heralded the arrival of the police car. I was glad the ambulance had been rather faster to arrive. As soon as they'd left the room, I slumped back down on the sofa. The bursar, with a brief pitying look at Joe, collected the empty mugs then marched purposefully out of the room, leaving Joe and me alone.

35

ALL'S FAIR IN LOVE AND CYCLING

There was an awkward silence.

'I'm not, you know,' said Joe at last. 'I'm not a cheat or a fraud. It's something I prefer not to talk about. What's past is past. But now I'd better tell you the whole truth.'

I said nothing but sat back to allow McPhee to jump on to my lap, where he nestled down and lay purring as Joe began to explain.

'There's a reason I had to leave cycling and take up teaching,' he said. 'But it's not what Steven thinks. You see, I was going out with my teammate's sister. Although he was talented, he was less devoted to his training regime than he should have been. He got called for a random urine test after he'd been out on the town one night, where he'd been indulging in some recreational drugs. He knew he had to take the test or he'd be off the team. His sister, my girlfriend, persuaded me to supply a specimen for him. Honestly, you'd think the security would be too tight to allow a substitution, but somehow we managed it. Mine, of course, was clear. I'm a clean-living lad.' He gave a feeble smile. 'But his performance started to fall off – hardly surprising considering that he wasn't living the lifestyle of a professional athlete – and his sister put pressure on me to pull some strings to keep a place on the team for him. But I was neither able nor willing, if he wasn't prepared to work for it.

'Then when he got kicked off the team, his dear sister persuaded him to make a clean sheet of his past by selling his lurid story to the tabloids. This included confessing to passing my specimen off as his own. God knows how she thought that would help anybody. I daresay it made him a bit of money initially, but it didn't put either of us in a very good light. I felt obliged to step down so as not to bring the whole team into disrepute.'

'That was very noble of you, Joe,' I said, feeling sorry for him now. 'Though completely unfair on you.'

He shrugged. 'Life isn't fair, really, is it? But I've landed on my feet, sort of. At least I've got a job.'

'But how on earth did you persuade Miss Harnett to take you on here, and to pretend you were a woman, to boot? There must be easier ways to earn a living.'

He shrugged again. 'Having had my name and reputation dragged through the gutter press, I think a hidey-hole like this, out of the public eye, suits me very well. Oriana was great pals with my ex-girlfriend and was incensed with how she and her brother treated me. She's got a big heart beneath her gold-digging outer shell. She was the one who persuaded Miss Harnett to give me a try. That was a couple of years ago, and, well, here I am still. For all its foibles, St Bride's keeps me safe from the prying eyes of the media, so I'm in no rush to move on.'

That made perfect sense.

'Do any of the other teachers know the whole story?'

He shrugged. 'I don't think so. Mavis thinks I got the job through being an old flame of Oriana's. I'm not, though. Not an old flame, nor a new flame, nor any kind of flame at all. We're just good friends. But I've let Mavis perpetuate that misconception... I didn't think I was ready for another relationship after the nightmare I went through with Eleanora and her wretched brother. So as the only eligible man on the staff—'

'Besides the bursar,' I teased. 'And Gerry, the housekeeper.'

'—I was keen to keep my relationships professional. Until you came along, anyway, so the issue hasn't arisen. Only Oriana and her mother know the real nature of our relationship.'

'Oriana's mother? Where does she feature in all this?'

He put his hand over his mouth. 'Oh, sorry, I forgot you didn't know about that. Promise me you'll keep it to yourself, won't you?'

Before he could elaborate, Miss Harnett came bustling in through the door, still wearing her coat, her car keys in her hand, and the penny dropped.

'Miss Harnett is Oriana's mother?' I whispered in shock.

As the headmistress swept over to us, McPhee leapt from my lap into her arms, and she hugged the cat to her chest for comfort. It was strange to see Miss Harnett looking anxious, when she was usually so calm and self-assured.

'I came back as quickly as I could when I got the bursar's text. How is my darling Olive now? And where is she?'

She stumbled over to Joe and he stood up to hug her, a gesture of familiarity that presumably wasn't allowed during term time. She rested against him for a moment, obviously consoled by his reassuring presence.

'They've taken her to hospital, Miss Harnett,' Joe said. 'Get the bursar to drive you there. You don't want to be driving yourself. You won't be able to concentrate with the worry. Make him wait and bring you home again, too.'

She nodded obediently and set McPhee down on the rug. 'I shall. It's good for him to feel useful. It doesn't happen often.'

She stepped back and squeezed Joe's hands before bending down to wrap me in her arms and kiss me on both cheeks.

'I understand I have you to thank for her timely rescue, my dear. I cannot thank you enough. I bless the day you joined St Bride's, I really do.'

I wasn't sure she'd feel the same way when she discovered my ex-boyfriend had been her daughter's attacker, but I didn't want to spoil the moment.

Then she threw her keys on the coffee table and hurried out of the room to search for the bursar, fastening the buttons on her coat as she went.

'Olive?' I said to Joe once the door had closed behind her. 'So her name's not really Oriana.'

'Yes, Olive,' said Joe. 'Oriana is what she prefers to call herself, rather than the name that her mother chose for her. Apparently, Miss Harnett had a craving for olives when she was pregnant.'

I slumped back against the sofa, struggling to take this all in. 'I'm glad my mum didn't adopt that strategy. When she was expecting me, she was mad about Marmite. So is Miss Harnett really Mrs Bliss?'

'No, she is Miss Harnett, Miss Caroline Harnett. And she is adamant that she will remain so, despite the bursar's chivalrous attempts for decades to persuade her to marry him, after the unfortunate fling she had with a middle-aged governor when she first came to teach here, fresh out of teacher training college, not long after she'd been a pupil here herself.'

'So Miss Harnett is the Caroline that Oriana warned me about.'

Joe nodded. 'I have to admit I feel a little sorry for the bursar. He loves Oriana like a daughter, having known her since before she was born, and having no wife or children of his own.'

'I know,' I said, without thinking. 'I've seen his shrine to her in his office.'

Joe grinned. 'Oh, those photos? Yes, poor bloke. But I'll say this much for him – he's certainly provided for Oriana and her mother, in a roundabout way. He persuaded the governors when the school was at its lowest ebb and wasn't commercially saleable to transfer ownership of the estate to Hairnet for just a pound. Ever since then she's been focused on building it back up to a viable business, and the bursar supports her as much as he can. Or as much as she'll let him. She sees him as a glorified butler.'

'So what happened to the governor who fathered Oriana? If he was middle-aged when she was conceived...' I shuddered. '...I suppose he must be dead by now.'

'Collapsed and died of a heart attack before Oriana – Olive – was even born. Fancy having a dead person on your birth certificate, eh? Rumour has it that poor Hairnet loved him so much that she arranged for him to be secretly buried in the second plinth in the mausoleum.'

'What? Is that even allowed?'

'The school belongs to her, so she can do what she likes. Besides, that's what mausoleums are for: places of burial. Why else do you think she spends so much time there? She's been loyal to him, you have to give her credit for that. Maybe that's one reason Hairnet will never abandon St Bride's. She couldn't bear to leave him behind. Nor will many of us. Yes, we all read the jobs section in *The Times Ed* each week, but we seldom apply. It would take bailiffs to turf us out of St Bride's, not job ads.'

'Yet you needed a new English teacher this term. What happened to the old one?'

'Ah.' Joe passed a hand over his face. 'I'll tell you another day, when you're feeling stronger.'

That suited me just fine.

'It's very sad, though. Miss Harnett's such a warm-hearted person with so much love to give. Yet she has no one apart from Olive – Oriana – to give it to, and can only do that behind closed doors. I guess that's why Oriana stays here – for her mother's sake.'

Joe grinned. 'You overestimate her selflessness. She's only staying here till she finds a better place to live. And in the meantime, she does happen to love maths and enjoy teaching.'

'But if, like Lady Bunting, she ever does find someone with a better mansion to share, poor Hairnet will be left on her own with only McPhee for comfort.' I stroked McPhee's head. I wasn't sure when he'd materialised on my lap again.

'Aren't you forgetting someone?' Joe nodded at the latest school photo that hung on the wall beside the head's desk. 'That's the biggest family photo I've ever seen.'

I followed his gaze. 'All the same, poor Oriana – how awful to have to pretend all the time that Miss Harnett isn't her mother, and to have spent no time at all with her father. That isn't how parental relationships should be.'

I bit my lip. It wasn't how mine should be either. I resolved to phone my parents that very evening. I didn't want to waste any more time before we were reconciled. They'd been right about Steven: he had never been worth it. I'd never let a man come between me and my parents again.

I got to my feet, thinking I should return to my flat.

'Anything else I need to know about before the staff and girls get back?' I asked, with a smile. 'Though really, I've had enough surprises for one day.'

'Well, you need to know how to keep a secret here, that's for sure.'

I grinned. 'What happens in the mausoleum, stays in the mausoleum?'

He nodded. 'I'm sure Oriana will be back in action shortly, doubtless with another new style.'

I thought for a moment. 'I can picture her as an Italian Mafia leader's moll next time: capri pants, sweater, and beret, with a big silk scarf around her neck till the bruising's come and gone.' I paused, relishing the image, then came back to reality. 'Do the other staff know about her relationship to Miss Harnett?'

'Oh yes, and they're happy to keep it under wraps, in return for their own secrets being kept. Take Mavis, for example.'

I froze. I'd just realised I hadn't yet cleared away the evidence of my inspection of the library.

'You've cottoned on to her game, I take it? Selling off old library books to fund her retirement?'

'I'm afraid so. But does Miss Harnett know? And the bursar? And do they mind?'

Joe shook his head. 'Not at all, because they have a deal. She's working her way through the whole stock. In return for the hours she's putting into the mind-numbing task of trawling through every book, she's allowed to keep the proceeds of any she flogs for less than ten quid. There are hundreds more in the cellars, too.'

'But the bursar told me there aren't any valuable books in the library. He didn't even mind when he found an old one with all the colour plates cut out.'

Joe shrugged. 'Different terms of reference. He would only consider one valuable if it was worth thousands of pounds, not tens. If he was paying Mavis or anyone else a commercial hourly rate for the work she's doing, it wouldn't break even. She does it for free on spec and works out the best way of earning money from each book. Mostly she sells the whole thing, but sometimes she can make much more by cutting out the colour plates and selling them to picture dealers. She spends hours and hours every week on the project. At this rate, it will take her till she's about ninety to work her way through the whole library.'

'She could speed it up tremendously if she dropped her

stubbornness and looked up prices on the internet,' I suggested. 'But you're right. Speed is not her priority. She doesn't want to complete the job because then the school might make her retire. It's like Homer's *Odyssey* all over again, with Penelope secretly unravelling the cloth at night that she weaves in the day in Odysseus's absence.'

Joe waved a hand dismissively. 'Don't try and baffle me with the classics, Miss Lamb. I'm a lost cause when it comes to culture.'

'No, but at least you can read,' I said, without thinking.

'You cheeky thing! Just because I prefer Dick Francis to Jane Austen doesn't make me illiterate.'

I suppressed a smile at the absurdity of my earlier fear that Joe might not be able to read. Not that it would have mattered to me if he had been illiterate. I'd have been happy to give him private reading lessons.

But Joe had more pressing things to tell me. 'Anyway, the deal is, when Mavis sells more valuable books, she has to reimburse the school. The bursar trusts her judgement and her honesty.'

'So that's why he was happy for me to help myself to old books without worrying about their value. I thought he just didn't realise they were worth anything. He asked me to run them past Mavis first, knowing she wouldn't let me cannibalise any that had resale value.'

Joe nodded. 'He's not as daft as people think, not least Oriana. And to be fair to him, it's been win-win so far: Mavis's dealings covered last term's electricity bill, for example, which is massive in a place like this. But we're under strict instructions to keep their arrangement quiet, otherwise the parents will expect us to reduce the fees, or at least to peg them. That's why I didn't want to tell you about it. Every time the school comes into money, like a legacy from an old girl, the wretched parents expect a cut of it. They don't realise how expensive it is to maintain a place like this. Apart from those who live in similar stately piles, of course. And they're the most penny-pinching of all because they're mostly broke from keeping up their own estates.'

'Mavis will be covering a lot more than the electricity bill with a book I spotted up there yesterday. I reckon it's worth over forty grand. I'm pretty sure there are others of similar value on the same shelf. I guess Mavis's survey hasn't reached that spot yet.'

Joe's eyes widened.

'A shelf full of books worth forty grand apiece? That'll be beyond Mavis's wildest dreams, and the bursar's too. A windfall like that will put a whole different tenor on the school's accounts, which, goodness knows, have been in a bad way for a while now. It might even persuade the bursar to turn the central heating on before half-term! My goodness, Gemma, not only have you saved Oriana today – you've also saved the school!'

I could hardly believe my good fortune.

'I'm guessing I can stop worrying now about whether I'll pass my probation.'

I was only half-joking, but the look on Joe's face told me all I needed to know.

'There was never any doubt of that, I'm sure. Now, Gemma, let's go fetch this valuable tome and show it to Hairnet the minute she gets back from the hospital. That'll take her mind off poor Oriana's injuries.'

He seized my hand to pull me to my feet and kept hold of it all the way to the library. As we entered the room, he raised our clasped hands and said, 'Make the most of this, you know. This is another secret we'll have to keep during term time. But it'll be half-term before you know it, and then we'll make up for lost time. That is, if you feel the same way...'

'Actually, I'm not sure I'm ready for another relationship yet either...'

But I let him take my other hand and draw me close to kiss me.

A gruff cough in the doorway made us leap apart.

'Looks like I'm going to have to impose another rule in the library,' said Mavis, stumping over to the blackboard and seizing a stub of chalk to add to the list. 'No kissing.'

But she was beaming encouragingly as Joe released me, and when I told her I'd come to show her the valuable book I'd found, she held the steps steady to keep me safe as I climbed up to the top shelf to fetch it.

* * *

'Nice exeat, girls?' I said, as I welcomed them into the entrance hall. The bursar had asked me to stand in for Oriana, who was taking a couple of days off in her mother's apartment until the worst of the bruising had subsided.

'Yes, thanks.'

'Lovely, miss.'

'It was top, miss.'

Then there was a silence.

'I expect it's been quiet without us. Did you miss us, miss?' Tilly looked hopeful.

'I've missed you all, of course,' I said, meaning it.

'It's nice to be back, miss,' said Imogen. 'Even though nothing ever happens here, it's always a nice nothing.'

'Yes,' I said. 'And let's hope it stays that way. Now, go to your dorms to unpack, then be down to supper in half an hour sharp.'

'Yes, miss,' they chorused, before bustling off towards the girls' stairs, chattering at the tops of their voices.

That just gave me time to write the postcard to my parents I'd been meaning to fit in this weekend, if I made a dash for my flat. As I ran lightly back up the marble staircase, I smiled to myself.

I hadn't touched the bannisters once.

ACKNOWLEDGMENTS

With grateful thanks to all those who helped, directly or indirectly, with the writing and production of this book:

Friends, former colleagues, and past pupils of Westonbirt School, where I worked for thirteen years in rather different circumstances from Gemma Lamb's. The strength and warmth of its community spirit inspired me to invent St Bride's.

Jane Reid, for allowing me to cite the two most useful things she'd learned at school.

Orna Ross, for telling me about the origins of the education system in the Russian Army.

My pre-publication readers Lucienne Boyce, Belinda Holley, and Belinda Pollard, who saved me from myself.

The editor of the first edition, Alison Jack.

My cover designer Rachel Lawston for the stunning cover and the series branding.

The editor of the first edition, Alison Jack.

My agent Ethan Ellenberg of Ethan Ellenberg Literary Agency for his wise counsel and encouragement.

The brilliant publishing team at Boldwood Books, including Tara Loder, Susan Lamprell, Madeleine Hamey-Thomas, and Emily Reader, for all their enthusiasm, energy, and expertise in creating this edition.

ALSO BY DEBBIE YOUNG

The Sophie Sayers Village Mysteries

Best Murder in Show

Trick or Murder?

Murder in the Manger

Murder by the Book

Springtime for Murder

Murder Your Darlings

Murder, Lost and Found

Staffroom at St Bride's Stories

Dastardly Deeds at St Bride's

Sinister Stranger at St Bride's

Scandal at St Bride's

Tales from Wendlebury Barrow *(quick reads)*

The Natter of Knitters

The Clutch of Eggs

MORE FROM DEBBIE YOUNG

We hope you enjoyed reading *Dastardly Deeds at St Bride's*. If you did, please leave a review.

If you'd like to gift a copy, this book is also available as an ebook, digital audio download and audiobook CD.

Sign up to Debbie Youngs' mailing list for news, competitions and updates on future books.

https://bit.ly/DebbieYoungNews

The next in the Gemma Lamb Cosy Mystery series, *Sinister Stranger at St Bride's*, is available to order now.

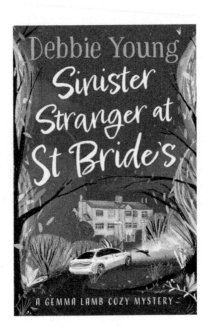

Debbie Young

Sinister Stranger at St Bride's

A GEMMA LAMB COZY MYSTERY

ABOUT THE AUTHOR

Debbie Young is the much-loved author of the Sophie Sayers and St Brides cosy crime mysteries. She lives in a Cotswold village, where she runs the local literary festival, and has worked at Westonbirt School, both of which provide inspiration for her writing.

Visit Debbie's Website: www.authordebbieyoung.com.

facebook.com/AuthorDebbieYoung

instagram.com/debbieyoungauthor

bookbub.com/authors/debbie-young

Boldwood

Boldwood Books is an award-winning fiction publishing company seeking out the best stories from around the world.

Find out more at www.boldwoodbooks.com

Join our reader community for brilliant books, competitions and offers!

Follow us
@BoldwoodBooks
@BookandTonic

Sign up to our weekly deals newsletter

https://bit.ly/BoldwoodBNewsletter

Printed in Great Britain
by Amazon